Stay With Me

Ashley Erin

Copyright © 2024 by Ashley Erin

Cover Design by Dana Leah

Image from Deposit Photos

Developmental Editing: M.E. Carter

Editing: Missy Borucki

Proofreading: Virginia Tesi Carey

Sensitivity Read: M. Park

Interior Design: Ashley Erin

All rights reserved. No part of this book may be reproduced or transmitted in any form or by any means, electronic or mechanical, including photocopying, recording, or by any information storage and retrieval system, without permission in writing.

No part of this work was generated or aided with the use of AI.

This is a work of fiction. Names, characters, places and incidents are the product of the author's imagination or are used fictitiously, and any resemblance to any actual persons, living or dead, events, or locales is entirely coincidental. The author acknowledges the trademarked status and trademark owners of various products referenced in this work of fiction, which have been used without permission. The publication/use of these trademarks is not authorized, associated with, or sponsored by the trademark owner. All rights reserved.

Contents

Dedication	V
1. Chapter One	1
2. Chapter Two	9
3. Chapter Three	17
4. Chapter Four	24
5. Chapter Five	33
6. Chapter Six	37
7. Chapter Seven	45
8. Chapter Eight	51
9. Chapter Nine	58
10. Chapter Ten	64
11. Chapter Eleven	69
12. Chapter Twelve	74
13. Chapter Thirteen	80
14. Chapter Fourteen	85
15. Chapter Fifteen	89

16.	Chapter Sixteen	97
17.	Chapter Seventeen	101
18.	Chapter Eighteen	106
19.	Chapter Nineteen	110
20.	Chapter Twenty	117
21.	Chapter Twenty-One	121
22.	Chapter Twenty-Two	127
23.	Chapter Twenty-Three	131
24.	Chapter Twenty-Four	137
25.	Chapter Twenty-Five	143
26.	Chapter Twenty-Six	149
27.	Epilogue	152

Dedicated to Nicole.

Your friendship means the world to me. Thank you for being excited to read my books.

Chapter One

Elise

The early summer sun is warm on my back as I paddle next to Young Jae. It's our Sunday tradition. I close Perk Up early, and we do something fun outdoors. At this time of year, it's usually paddle boarding on Willowbrook Lake or going for a hike. In the winter, we go snowshoeing or snowboarding.

A chance to hang out with my best friend is the highlight of every week. Especially since home has been an endless cycle of false promises and bickering. That is when Jake bothers to acknowledge me at all. More often he sits scrolling his phone with the TV on as background noise.

Young Jae splashes at me with his paddle, the cold water hitting my shins. He chuckles at my yelp of surprise. "You seem distracted today, you good?"

Sighing, I nod. "Yeah, it's nothing new." He looks unconvinced, so I change the subject. "I'm thinking about expanding the menu at Perk Up to include hot dishes offered at dinnertime. I don't fully know how to make it work though, unless I hire someone."

His eyes light up. He's been telling me to hire some help for years. "That sounds like a great idea. It would increase business to allow you to do those upgrades, and once they're trained, you would have more free time."

Free time. Something I lack unless I make the decision to close early. I put in thirteen-to-fourteen-hour days, five days a week, with Sundays being a little shorter at around ten hours. It's a lot, but I love my café and couldn't imagine doing anything else. The long days also help keep me busy and distracted from things I'm only just starting to admit to myself. Home isn't a fun place to be and my relationship with Jake has been lackluster on the best days for a couple of years now. I purposely stay as on the go as possible. Mondays are my only day off because Perk Up is closed on Mondays.

"That's true. I have been thinking it would be nice to keep more regular hours. Adeline has such a great balance at the shelter, and with Rae shifting into her new career, it will also free up her time. Maybe it's time I consider the next steps of my business as well." I'm thinking out loud, off in la-la land. "I could put out an ad at the very least."

"Do it. You don't have to hire anyone if you don't find the right fit. Besides, then you won't have to put the 'back in five' sign up every time you need to use the bathroom." Young Jae's smile is brilliant, showing off the dimple in his left cheek. "You've built Perk Up into the incredible shop it is. I know it's hard to allow someone else in, but it's a good thing. You have worked so hard to get here. I'm proud of you."

His words mean so much to me, but he's always encouraged me when it comes to Perk Up, right from when he helped redesign the building for me, drafting the plans for free.

Grinning in return, his expression is all the encouragement I need. If I want Perk Up to grow, I need to consider hiring someone. It's hard to open my business up to a new person, but if they were the right person, it wouldn't be a bad thing.

Before I can say anything, his phone rings.

He answers as soon as he sees the name on the screen. "Hey, man. What's up?"

As he chats, his voice gets more excited, and I grab my phone to check the time.

Deflating when I realize what time it is, I tuck my phone back into my waterproof pouch as Young Jae ends his call.

"I have something I want to show you. Let's head in." His brown eyes are practically twinkling he's so excited.

Frowning, I apologize. "I'm sorry. I wish I could, but Jake promised we would have a date night tonight. I need to get home."

His face tightens slightly, but he nods. I know he doesn't like Jake. Most of my girlfriends don't either. I quit wishing Jake would make more of an effort with my friends years ago. He never had any interest in getting to know my circle. He keeps to his group and says he's happy to let me spend time with my friends without him.

"Okay, I guess you'll find out next week." His tone is mischievous, taunting.

Pouting, I give him my best sad face. "You're not going to tell me?"

"Nope. You're gonna have to wait." He chuckles at my expression, paddling toward the shore.

Following behind, I wonder if Jake will be ready for our night out. He tends to lose track of time on his phone or crash without setting an alarm. Pondering whether I can be a little late so I can check out what Young Jae wants to show me, I huff out a heavy sigh. I can't do that. It's not me to disregard a prior arrangement.

I'm so distracted in my thoughts that by the time my gaze catches Young Jae's board angling as he adjusts his course, it's too late to avoid his board.

"Shit! Incoming!" I dig my paddle in to try and slow down as we collide.

My foot slips, and I teeter on my board before tumbling into the water.

Spluttering as I surface, the sound of laughter is the first thing I hear. Scowling playfully, I push my hair out of my face before splashing up at him. "Very funny."

"It was. Your arms windmilled like a cartoon character." He drops down to sit on his board, holding mine steady as I crawl out of the water, his body shaking with unrestrained laughter as I sit up, water dripping down my body.

Young Jae's laughter cuts off as he glances at me before darting his gaze away. Clearing his throat, he gestures at me. "Your shirt is see-through."

His accent is thicker than normal, making me pause before I glance down and realize that not only is it see-through, but the bra I'm wearing is also transparent.

"Oh my god!" Pulling my shirt away from my body helps, but the busy dock will still get an eye full.

"Here." Young Jae pulls his shirt over his head, sticking his arm out without looking. The muscles of his back are prominent as he holds his shirt, waiting for me.

Taking it, I pull it over my head. It smells like him. I inhale deeply before I can stop myself. The fabric is warm from his body heat, warming me as the shirt drapes loosely around me. "Thank you. You can turn around again."

It's a good thing I'm not prone to blushing because I'm positive I would be scarlet as his gaze locks on mine. The silence pulses between us.

Glancing away, I move to stand, careful so I don't go plunging into the lake again. "We better go. I need to shower now."

He looks at his watch, nodding. A muscle in his cheek twitches, but when he looks at me again, his face is relaxed, an easy grin on his lips. "And I need to go pick something up. Something you will love but need to wait to see."

Shaking my head, I mutter, "Tease."

We paddle back to the dock without another incident, the weirdness passing as we load our paddleboards.

"Have fun tonight." Young Jae smiles as he opens his car door. "I will talk to you later."

"I will." Waving as he drives away, I wring my hair out before getting into my car and heading to Jake's house. We've been together for over five years, and despite moving into his home three years ago, it's never quite felt like ours. Maybe it's because that's when our issues seemed to start.

Parking next to Jake's truck, I hop out and glance at the time. Jake promised he would be ready for when I got home, so even with a quick shower we can leave as planned.

Opening the door, I call out, "I'm home." The words cut off abruptly as I trip on Jake's shoes, laying in the middle of the floor. Again.

Closing my eyes, I inhale slowly through my nose, holding the breath and then releasing slowly. It's fine. It's not a big deal.

I put his shoes away and then mine. It's an argument we've had countless times, but I'm not going to fight with him about it today. It's date night.

Hanging up my stuff, I wander through the house to the kitchen, stopping dead in my tracks. It looks like a bomb went off when it was spotless this morning. Jake had the day off and I knew he would make himself food, but he didn't bother to clean up after himself in the slightest. Pressing my lips together, I turn around and head to the living room.

Jake is laying on the couch, scrolling his phone, wearing sweats and a ratty T-shirt. The coffee table has more dishes and wrappers from other food.

"Hey," I greet him, leaning against the wall. He doesn't respond, scrolling away. "Jake!"

He finally glances away from his phone, brows pinched. "Oh, hi." Jake barely glances at me, missing the fact I'm soaked and wearing an oversized T-shirt. His eyes are automatically back to his phone. "You're home early."

Planting my hands on my hips, I bite out, "I'm home right on time. We're supposed to be going out for date night. You told me you'd make reservations."

Jake sits up, finally turning his attention from his phone to me. "Oh yeah. I forgot. Let's just go to Cliff's."

My chest tightens. "Don't worry about it. I'm going to shower, and I guess clean up the house."

He stands up, groaning. "I said I'm sorry."

"Yep. And?"

"Why are you being like this?" Jake rolls his eyes, returning his attention to the stupid device he is constantly attached to.

The anger simmering boils over at that question. "Because you're constantly disregarding me and anything that's important to me. You barely look at me. Barely spend time with me. You basically treat me like a live-in maid that you get to have sex with."

His eyes widen, jaw set as he scowls. "That's a load of crap."

"Don't gaslight me. How many times have I asked you to put your shoes away? How many times have I requested that you do something to help keep this house clean?" Gesturing around me and the mess that wasn't present when I left for work this morning, I practically growl, "You've been home all day and somehow didn't have time to clean up after yourself. So not only did you forget you promised me you'd be ready for date night, but also left a mess for me to come home to after I stayed up late last night cleaning the house."

"It will take me ten minutes to get ready. Why are you bitching when you also need to get ready? And I will get around to cleaning." His voice is exasperated, and it grinds on my last nerve.

"You've got to be fucking joking. No, you would leave the mess for me to take care of because I always do." Gesturing to myself, I pull at the shirt. "And yeah, I need to get ready, but with both of us needing the bathroom, it clogs it up."

He stands, knocking a chip bag onto the floor, which he ignores. "Wow. You just have impossibly high standards. Are we going to go to Cliff's or not?"

Jake moves to brush past me, continuing to ignore the chip bag on the floor. I've had enough.

"No. We're not. I'm done. I can't keep having these same conversations over and over. It's senseless when you clearly have a blatant disregard for how I feel." Crossing my arms, I hold his gaze. "It's over. I will pack some things for now and come back tomorrow for the rest of my belongings."

He gapes at me. "Are you serious? Because I forgot date night?"

Scoffing, I press my fingers into my temples before staring at him incredulously. "If that's what you need to think. I'm not wasting any more of my breath trying to help you understand."

I turn, head to the bedroom, and pack some things into a bag. Enough to get me through the night. My entire body is calm, accepting. I thought there would be sadness, a question about whether this is the right choice, but nothing comes. Just relief. This has been a long time coming, but I just kept making excuses or feeling sad about the time devoted to a dead-end relationship.

Somewhere along the way I think I grieved this before I even knew it was a done deal.

Glancing around the room, there's a small bookshelf that holds my books and that's about it. The rest of the space is missing my personal touch. It doesn't even feel like I'm saying goodbye to my space, my home. It feels like I'm leaving a hotel room I stayed in for a while.

I walk past Jake, who's still standing bewildered in the middle of the living room, for the book I've been reading before passing him again and going to the door. Without a word, I slide my feet back into my shoes, grab the rest of the things I need from the closet, and head out the door.

Mindlessly I get in my car and drive. I did it. I can't believe I did it. I've been thinking about ending my relationship with Jake for the past year, seriously considering it but struggling to take the leap. I don't know what finally clicked, but I know that nothing is going to change, and I want a relationship like I see my friends have.

Owen dotes on Adeline, their love story one from the movies. And Cam and Rae, the way they found their way back to each other and managed to work through what felt impossible. Seeing them listen to each other and work on their relationship was the clarity I needed.

If Jake wanted to, he would've made the effort.

I didn't even think about where to go, my body automatically bringing me here.

Parking my car, I stare at Young Jae's house. The two-story is beautiful. I remember when he was designing this house, updating me as he worked and reworked until it was just right.

My clothes rub against me as I get out of my car. Shivering, I hope Young Jae is home. Even though I have a spare key, I would feel too weird to go inside and have a shower.

Ringing the bell, all the tension leaves my body when he opens the door, hair tousled and looking a little sleepy. His brows crease when he sees my bags and still wet clothes.

"I left Jake. Ended things. I'm just . . . done." My voice is soft. And it feels weird to say those words without the emotion that usually comes with them. He stripped me of the last ounce of regard I had for our relationship.

Young Jae opens the door wide, stepping to the side. His tone is soft as he says, "Stay with me."

Chapter Two

Elise

Stepping into Young Jae's house, I sigh. My shoulders drop, the tension easing immediately, and the air feels clearer in my lungs. He shuts the door behind me, taking my bags.

"Make—" His words are cut off by a white blur wriggling at my feet.

Gaping, I stare down at an adorable Jack Russell Terrier. "Oh. My. God. Who is this?"

Dropping down, I pull the wriggling bundle of energy into my arms, giggling as the dog licks my neck.

"That's Kimchi. She's what I wanted to show you earlier." Young Jae grins as I plop onto my butt, petting the excited dog. "She was dropped off as a stray at the vet clinic around a month ago. Cam tried to find the owner without success. So after getting some weight on her and taking care of some medical issues, I told him I wanted to adopt her."

Kimchi curls up in my lap, huffing out a sigh as I stroke between her ears. "I've always wanted a Jack Russell," I whisper.

"I know. I wanted to give her to you, but I remember you mentioning a couple years ago that Jake didn't want a dog." His voice is carefully neutral, which I appreciate in this moment. I don't want to think about Jake. "Since you're here, I want you to think of her as yours too."

"I can't believe you remember that." Tears fill my eyes as I hunch over her and bury my face into her neck. Wiping my face, the dampness of my sleeve reminds me I still haven't showered or changed.

Lifting Kimchi, I stand, slipping out of my shoes and putting them into the shoe rack by the door. I give her one last hug before setting her on the floor. Gesturing at Young Jae's shirt, still warming me, I grimace. "I could use a hot shower."

Young Jae grins. "Consider the bedroom across from mine as yours, the one with the full bathroom attached."

Giving him a grateful look, I take my bag from him and head upstairs to the room. My room.

The bedroom is spacious, even with a queen-sized bed. It's beautifully made with emerald-colored bedding. The walls are a deep forest green, the dark color calming. I admire the tasteful bedside lamps and set my bag down on the window seat. Opening the closet, I can't help but sigh dreamily at the size. It's a deep walk-in with custom built shelving. It's been ages since I came upstairs, not since Young Jae moved in four years ago, and I forgot how amazing the closets are.

Not bothering to unpack, I grab some clean clothes and my toiletries. The bathroom is also large, with an oversized shower and plenty of counter space. Pulling at the damp shirt, I close my eyes for a moment and sigh. Eager to wash the day away, I strip down and go to turn on the water.

Gaping as I finally take in the luxury that is the shower, I stare at the spa wall. The multitude of buttons are intimidating, but it doesn't take long until I'm standing under the warmth of water from four different directions.

The heat eases the remaining tension from my shoulders. Reality sinking in as I process what happened. I can't believe I did it. I've been through break-ups before, but none of my previous relationships were ever going to go anywhere. Jake and I discussed marriage at one point, and he said he wanted to start a family. Kids has always been something I'm on the fence about. I was okay having them, but I was also perfectly content to have a childfree life. He was always the one to bring it up, but then never seemed serious about the things that actually led to that.

When did that all change? I can't really pinpoint the time, but it's been a long time.

Despite my relief, my heart grieves the time I sacrificed for a relationship that had no future. If I'm being honest with myself, I ignored a lot of red flags from early on because he promised me the things I wanted.

Tilting my head back, letting the water stream over me, I wash the day away. No part of me really feels sad at the loss of Jake, the shame and guilt at admitting that quick to surface. He's not a bad guy, but he has a lot of growing to do to be a good partner.

Finishing my shower, I pull on my shorts, sports bra, and an oversized T-shirt. Staring at the big bed, I relish the idea of spreading out in it. Maybe I can convince Young Jae to let Kimchi sleep with me.

My stomach growls loudly, reminding me that my dinner plans fell through. I towel dry my hair, brushing it quickly before heading downstairs.

The only sound in the house is the TV. Following it, I pause at the sight before me. There is a smorgasbord of food on the coffee table, and Young Jae is sprawled out on his couch, some action movie playing, but he is scrolling the channels.

"This is a ton of food," I finally say, stepping into the room.

He glances at me, his gaze dropping to my legs before jolting back to my eyes, a smirk on his lips. "I figured you would be hungry but I didn't know what you'd want, so I ordered your favorites."

Plopping onto the other side of his sectional, I peruse the food. The red curry wins first pick, so I snag it. "You're the best. Thank you for making this easy."

"You know I'd do anything for you." He clears his throat, gesturing to the TV. "What do you want to watch?"

He continues to scroll through as I eat.

"Oh! *Rogue One*!" My mouth is full, but I don't want him to miss it.

Young Jae selects it but laughs. "Haven't you watched this half a dozen times?"

"At least, but I love it."

He sits up, helping himself to some food. Offering him the red curry, he scoops some out onto his plate.

We don't say much as we eat and watch. The silence is easy and comfortable.

"Do you think I could steal Kimchi to snuggle tonight?" I finally ask after setting down the empty takeout container.

"Of course. Any time. She's a bed hog though, and loves to crawl under the covers to snuggle. We were just having a nap, and I didn't know a little dog could take up so much room." His voice is affectionate as he warns me, petting the dog that's sound asleep next to him.

Chuckling, I stretch out, my stomach protesting at how full it is. The coffee table looks like we had a group of frat boys visiting—everything is gone. Groaning as I stand, I start to tidy the table.

"What're you doing? Relax. I've got this." Young Jae motions for me to sit, his expression brooking no room for argument.

Pulling a blanket over me, I smile. "You're the best."

He cleans up as I watch the movie, rejoining me as we get to the end. I don't bother hiding my tears as the main leads hold each other, waiting for their end.

Young Jae hands me a tissue. "It's cute that you still cry for this scene."

"They went through so much to get there, only to lose it all." Sniffling, I wipe my nose. Glancing at the time, I begrudgingly get up and fold the blanket. "I guess I better head to bed. I need to pack up the rest of my stuff tomorrow while Jake is at work. Thank you again, I appreciate you."

He stands as I do, pulling me into a hug. His arms are solid around me as I lay my head on his chest. The steady thump of his heart beating against my ear. "I'm here for you. All I want is your happiness."

"Hangbokhae." Telling him I'm happy in Korean, one of the first things I learned when he taught me, makes him smile. Stepping away, I look up at him and beam. "Jal ja." I say goodnight and head upstairs.

"Kimchi, come!" Calling her from the landing, I wait as she runs up the stairs, her stumpy tail wagging.

Closing the door to my room, I wash up before crawling into bed. Exhaling as I snuggle in, Kimchi finds her way behind my knees. I envelop myself in the covers and smile. This bed is a dream and despite the happenings of the day, I feel okay, and that says everything about where I was at.

Picking up my phone, I set an alarm for seven a.m. before checking my messages. My group chat with the girls is quiet, but I didn't tell the gals about the break-up so it's not unexpected. I will message them tomorrow. But there are a couple messages from Jake.

Jake: Are you seriously not coming back? I cleaned up the kitchen. We can have a date night tomorrow. I didn't realize it was that important to you.

Jake: Baby, we've been together for five years. How can you just spring this on me?

Barking out a laugh, I set my phone to do not disturb and lay it on the nightstand. Spring it on him? It goes to show how little he paid attention to the things I've said.

Taking a deep breath, I run through a to-do list in my mind until I finally start to doze off.

***

Parking outside Jake's house shortly after ten, I'm relieved to see his truck is gone. When I woke this morning to more texts telling me he would change, I worried he would be waiting for me.

I take a deep breath before opening my door and getting out. Seeing the house doesn't make me feel sad. It's almost unnerving how at peace I feel, but I'm relieved that the decision has been easier than I had told myself it would be for the past year.

A vehicle pulls in next to me as I grab boxes and packing tape from my trunk. I tense, closing my eyes to prepare myself for what's sure to be an awkward encounter. I give myself a mental squeeze before straightening to see who is there.

Owen grins at me from his open door. Gripping the back of my car, I sag in relief. "Oh my god, Owen, I was prepping for an awkward encounter with Jake."

"Nah. Young Jae texted this morning to rally the troops. Adeline is following behind. She wanted to bring you food. Raelynn and Cam should be here shortly with Rae's truck." He pauses, glancing behind me. "And Young Jae just pulled up."

Turning, I press my hand over my heart. I love my friends.

Young Jae hops out, grinning as he digs around and comes up with more boxes. "We're not letting you do this on your own."

"You guys are the best." I smile, grateful.

Owen takes the boxes, and we head into the house. I've read enough stories online to be relieved that Jake didn't change the locks, but based on his texts, I'm not overly surprised.

What does surprise me is the fact that the house is actually clean.

I come to a full stop in the kitchen. It's spotless. And it's never looked like this when I wasn't the one who cleaned it.

Young Jae comes to my shoulder, murmuring, "Once doesn't mean change."

Turning, I nod my agreement. "I know. It's too late."

"Where do you want me to start?" Owen comes in.

I direct him and Young Jae to the living room for my books and a few pictures. I turn as the remainder of our group comes in, more boxes in hand. Adeline leads the way with a cake and carafe of coffee.

"I know I'm not the expert, but I wanted to provide sustenance." Adeline sets everything down on the table, turning to take to-go cups and plates from a bag that Raelynn is carrying.

They open their arms and I rush in for a hug. "I'm sorry I didn't message you yesterday. I just wanted to land and process."

Rae scoffs. "Why are you apologizing? We're just glad Young Jae had the sense to ask for help."

Laughing, I pull away and start delegating tasks. I don't have much, so once we clear out the closet and the rest of my things from the bathroom, grab the few appliances I added to Jake's kitchen, and my stash of books and odd knickknacks, we're done in less than two hours.

Eating cake in the house I'm moving out of feels too weird, so we all head back to Young Jae's house.

By the time all my boxes are in Young Jae's garage, we're all starving. Owen offers to go to Cliff's for burgers as we pile into the living room.

"Oh my gosh, who is this?" Adeline coos at Kimchi, who is wriggling between all of us after being freed from her room. Young Jae turned his third empty bedroom into a dog room for her so she has space to roam when she's alone, but not so much to get into a lot of mischief.

"Kimchi," Young Jae and I say in unison.

We settle in the living room, playing with Kimchi as I fill in Rae and Adeline on what happened yesterday.

"I just looked around me and realized that he'd been taking me for granted for years and it was never going to get any better. And I realized I couldn't do it anymore. I gave him way too many chances because of the time we had together." Giving them a smile, I emphasize, "It was the best choice I could've made. Probably one I should've made sooner."

Rae squeaks a toy, throwing it for Kimchi. "You needed to get there on your own. I'm glad you feel good about it."

Owen comes in, laying out burgers on the table before presenting a bottle of champagne.

Adeline raises her brows at the bottle. "Champagne?"

"We're celebrating. Look at Elise. When was the last time you saw her looking so rested and relaxed?" Owen gestures at me. "Champagne was necessary."

"Um, I'm right here." Pointing at myself, I laugh. "But you're right, I do feel relaxed."

We all chow down, demolishing the burgers before Young Jae pops the champagne and Adeline cuts the cake. By the time everyone leaves it's late and I'm absolutely wiped. Somehow an afternoon celebration morphed into the evening as well. More food ordered and more champagne flowed. Despite the exhaustion, my heart is full.

Saying goodnight, I head upstairs with Kimchi on my heels.

I've left my phone on do not disturb all day, but I take it out of my pocket to see a string of messages from Jake.

Scanning them, they're more of the same from last night, but I don't respond.

Kimchi snuggles against me and, for the second night in a row, I fall asleep without anxiety keeping me up.

Chapter Three

Young Jae

Startled awake by a loud sound, I hear Elise whisper yell, "Ouch. Shit that hurt."

Her footsteps fade as she goes downstairs and I glance at my phone to check the time.

4:45 a.m.! My eyes practically bug out of my head. It never dawned on me how early Elise wakes to get to Perk Up and have everything ready for her 7:00 a.m. open time.

Groaning, I roll out of bed and pull on some shorts and a T-shirt. May as well make her breakfast and start my day too. I wash up in the bathroom before padding down the stairs. Elise is standing by the back door, waiting for Kimchi to be done doing her business.

She doesn't notice me, looking rested as she smiles at whatever antics Kimchi is getting into. Elise was beautiful as a teenager when we met, but she is stunning as a woman. Her quiet confidence is alluring.

Running my hand through my hair, I give my head a shake. I shouldn't be noticing how attractive or appealing she is. I locked those feelings up years ago.

"Morning." My voice is rough with sleep.

Elise jumps, turning with her hand pressed into her chest. "You scared the crap out of me. I wasn't expecting to see you this early."

"Not used to the extra sounds in the house," I rumble, my voice groggy from sleep. Heading into the kitchen, I scrub my hands down my face. Coffee. I need coffee. Turning on the coffee pot, I'm grateful I had the foresight to prep it last night. It doesn't take long for me to throw together breakfast for us. Using some leftover bulgogi, I make a Korean-style breakfast bowl.

Elise lets Kimchi in before pouring coffee and setting the table. Despite the early hour, I admit having her here in the morning is nice. Glancing at her, I appreciate that she's wearing jeans and a flowery top instead of her typical evening attire. I've always found her attractive, but seeing her dressed down is inexplicably hot. It's opened my eyes to seeing her in a way I've never had the chance to before. A way that I don't need to be looking at my best friend.

"I'm sorry I woke you. I bashed my funny bone on the hall table. It jumped out at me, I swear." She chuckles softly. "Thank you for breakfast."

Mumbling a "no problem," I devour my food still half asleep. Sipping at my coffee while I wait for her to finish, I ponder how I'm going to pass several extra hours of awake time.

As I move to clean up, she holds out her hand to stop me. "You cooked, I clean. It's only fair. You saved me time making breakfast, and I would've cleaned up after myself anyway."

It's useless to argue with Elise, so I move into the living room and call Kimchi to my lap. I never had any pets as a child. My parents were so busy in Korea working that they didn't want the responsibility. And that continued when we moved here. They didn't see the value in an animal when there was so much work to do and school to focus on.

As Kimchi curls on my lap, sighing contentedly as I pet her, I can't believe I waited fifteen years since becoming an adult to get a dog.

Elise finishes in the kitchen, coming out to stand by the hall. "I'm off. I should be home by eight-thirty if cleanup and prep goes well."

"I'll have something ready for dinner," I reply. "And don't forget to put up that ad. You're still planning on hiring someone, right?"

She smiles at me. "Yes. I'm still going to post for someone. It's time."

"Good."

Taking out my phone as she leaves, I scroll a bit but lose interest. I don't have to work for close to four hours, my normal wake-up time usually seven or eight, my work day not until nine.

Glancing around my living room and at all my stuff, I think about the boxes Elise has stored in my garage. She really didn't have too much to pack, which enraged me in a way I wasn't expecting. She lived in Jake's house for years, how does she have so little?

"Kimchi, what do you say we make space for Elise's stuff?" Scratching her head, I gently move her to the couch and stand. She looks at me and turns in a circle a few times before laying down with a huff. Shaking my head, I give her one more scratch. "You rest, I will get the boxes."

It doesn't take me long to bring in the boxes that belong in the main part of the house. I know Elise is planning to look for an apartment, but vacancies are always hard to come by in town, and I want her to know she's welcome to stay for as long as she needs.

Opening the boxes with her books, they definitely take up the most space. Pondering my shelves, I'm grateful for the built-ins I added on either side of my fireplace. I think if I move some of my stuff, I can fit all of her books.

I work quickly trying to remember how she organized her books, but as I step back and examine my handiwork, it just doesn't look right. Sighing, I grab my cell from the coffee table and call Ari.

"Why are you awake this early?" Her tone is a mixture of worry and suspicion.

"Cliffs notes: Elise moved in after she and Jake broke up and she wakes up at the ass crack of dawn." I adjust some of the books and still don't think it looks nice like how she had them. "Anyway, I'm not used to the noise of someone in my house; therefore, I also woke up abhorrently early."

"Wait, wait, wait. The woman you've secretly been in love with for seventeen years is living with you?" She sounds much perkier.

"I'm not in love—"

She cuts me off. "Whatever. Why are you calling this early?"

I massage the bridge of my noise. This was a mistake. Maybe I should just hang up.

"Young Jae!" Her voice is so shrill even Kimchi lifts her head in disgust.

Sighing, I mutter, "I was trying to unpack her books to surprise her, and they don't look nice like she had them..."

"Say no more." Ari hangs up.

With a groan, I head to the kitchen to make fresh coffee. I have plenty of time until I need to start my day, I should've just kept working at it. The early hour has clearly messed with my brain to make me ask Ari for her help. I love my sister, but she can be so meddlesome.

Our older brother lives a couple hours away, so I bear the brunt of her younger sister quirks.

Kimchi barks as my door swings open, banging into the doorstop.

"Annyeong, Oppa," she singsongs as she breezes into the house. She freezes when Kimchi rushes up and jumps on her before squealing and dropping to the floor. "I see there's more than one secret you've been keeping."

"No secrets, I just got her on Sunday. It's now Tuesday, calm down," I tease.

Ari rolls her eyes, rubbing Kimchi's belly as she looks at the bookshelves with Elise's books added. "Yikes. It's a good thing you called me."

She reluctantly gets up and pulls the books I've just added off the shelves. "Does she have any knickknacks?"

"Yeah, in the garage." I go grab the boxes with knickknacks—there's only two—and bring them in. "The rest of the stuff is her clothes and a few other items she had stored in her bedroom."

My sister scans the boxes and the stacks of books. "I'm glad she dumped his ass. Although, I've already heard rumblings through town that he's trying to win her back."

Scoffing, I growl, "Why wouldn't he? He took advantage of her and now he has to do everything himself."

"I mean, yes. But I do think he loves her, just not in the way she needs." She turns, her brown eyes somber. "She deserves someone who will cherish her... someone who will call their nosey sister to ask for help setting up a bookshelf."

I groan. "Don't start. We're just friends."

"Fine. Tell yourself whatever lies you need to." She returns to work, opening the boxes of little trinkets and ornaments that Elise had and adding them alongside books. "Ji Hoon called Mom last night. He's coming back to town for good. Eomma is over the moon."

Shock fills me. I'm close with Ji Hoon, we talk every day, and he never mentioned it to me. "Are you sure for good?"

She nods. "Yep. Bought the old auto shop. Said his friend and him are going to fix it up and open a garage. Will be nice not having to drive to Thistle Creek to get my car worked on."

"I wonder why he didn't tell me." Frowning, I move to help Ari by pulling the rest of Elise's things out of the boxes and clearing the cardboard out of the way. "Want some coffee? I made a fresh pot."

She nods, so I head to the kitchen, topping up my mug and making her a cup.

"Probably because he knew you would offer to design something or rush over there to help him move and he doesn't want to burden you." She turns, taking the cup with a firm look. "You always try to help everyone except yourself."

"That's not true." My tone is weak because I know she's not completely wrong. "I do things for myself, but there's nothing wrong with helping people."

Ari drops down to the floor, drinking her coffee. Her face is pensive. "No, there isn't. But I know you need more in your life. I hear how you talk about Owen and Cam and what they have. And I see how you look at Elise." She lifts her hand when I open my mouth to argue. "Whatever, you can deny it, but that woman has been the center of your world since high school. And if you think that Jake's ineptness as a boyfriend is the only reason that relationship didn't work out, then you're dumb."

Blindsided, I don't respond. I did have a crush on Elise when I first moved here. She helped me study English nearly every day. From there we became best friends and when I no longer needed her to study with, I was planning on asking her out and then Matthew "with two Ts" asked her out and she said yes.

It gutted me. There has been the odd occasion I've thought about crossing that boundary, but when she started dating Jake, I decided to move past my crush and cherish our friendship. Something I plan on sticking to.

"Done." Ari's voice startles me. "I think she's going to love it."

She stands back, admiring her handiwork and I have to admit, it looks amazing. "Wait, did you redo my books too?"

"Yeah, they've been bugging me for years." She smiles slyly. "Now should I check to see if you're keeping it a secret that you're together?"

I don't move as she bolts up the stairs, only to come down moments later looking disappointed.

Laughing, I shake my head. "Why don't you worry about your own damn love life instead of prying into my non-existent one?"

She crinkles her nose in disgust. "No one in town is interesting enough for me. And I don't plan on moving. So unless I take Eomma's offer to set me up with one of her friends' sons and they fly him out here, I will live vicariously through you."

She plops down on the couch, her lips drooping a little as we drink coffee in silence. It's unusual for Ari to allow silence to fill the air. Usually she's talking about anything and everything.

"You okay?"

Ari sighs, her lips pressing together as she meets my gaze. "I tried to talk to Eomma and Appa about retiring. Appa didn't say much, but Eomma and I argued. It sucks. They should retire, they've been working for so long. And I'm ready to run the inn on my own. Try some new things. But I can't keep arguing with Eomma about it."

I can't imagine being in her shoes. I know how stubborn our parents can be, especially our mother. Working with them has had its ups and downs, but mostly it's gone well, but Eomma always wants to take the lead on things and it's time for her to let Ari take the reins.

"Do you want me to talk to her?" The offer is genuine, but part of me hopes she will say no.

Ari's spine straightens, her eyes lighting up. "You would do that?"

Taking a deep breath, I nod. "Yes. Maybe an outside perspective will help."

She's bouncing on the spot now, her bright smile back. "You are the best big brother. Well, tied for best because Ji Hoon said he'd fix my car for free once the shop is running."

Lips twitching, I shake my head and roll my eyes.

She starts talking about me and Elise, her focus returning from her life to mine, when my alarm rings, alerting me to the time. With a hint of relief, I say, "I gotta get ready for work. Thanks for your help."

"Anytime, Oppa."

Chapter Four

Elise

The bell above the door jingles, announcing a customer. Glancing at the time, I grimace. Quarter to seven. With only fifteen minutes to closing, my shop is pretty picked over. At least Jake didn't show up today, maybe he will drop us getting back together.

Turning with a smile, it grows when I see Adeline. "Hey! Just finish work?"

"Yeah, we had a late intake and I stayed to help." She steps aside, revealing Brynne. "I convinced Brynne to come get a treat, it was a rough one."

I manage to contain my surprise when I see Brynne. Her auburn hair is pulled back in a ponytail, her tattooed arms covered by her leather jacket. Brynne tends to keep a low profile around town due to her family. Her brothers are in and out of jail. Her eldest brother is currently back in prison due to breach of parole. Her dad is an abusive jerk. And I'm pretty sure they have ongoing illegal activity on their run-down farm.

Despite living in town as soon as she could escape her family, I think she feels ashamed sharing the same DNA as them, typically keeping to herself. Aside from the shelter and grabbing necessities, she rarely ventures out.

"Hey, Brynne. It's nice to see you." I genuinely mean it. She's a nice woman, a little rough around the edges, but her heart is warm.

She gives me a small smile in return. "Hi." Her raspy voice takes me back to school, she would show up bruised and dirty. It took one boy to get his ass whooped by her for everyone to learn to steer clear and give Brynne as much space as possible. I never did though. It hurt too much seeing someone so mistreated.

"I don't have much left, but I did save some things just in case." While they sit down, I go to the back to grab the chocolate cannolis I made earlier. They are a test batch for the new menu items and I was going to bring them all home for Young Jae, but the recipe made way too many.

Bringing them out, I set them onto two of the hand-painted plates I picked up at the thrift store before delivering them to their table.

"Can I bring you some coffee too?"

"Oh wow! This looks amazing." Adeline looks up at me. "New recipe?"

Tucking my chin down, I smile. "Yeah. I want to expand the menu. I just posted a position for an evening staffer who can cook too."

"That's incredible, good luck! These look amazing, and I'm always happy to be a test subject. I would love a latte please." She glances at Brynne who is staring at the cannoli.

"I don't think I've ever eaten anything so pretty before." Her voice is soft. "I would love a hot chocolate. I remember how delicious yours is."

She looks up at me, her green eyes shimmering with remembrance.

Smiling at her, I nod. "Coming right up."

It makes me sad how much she has isolated herself. I'm glad Adeline thought to get her out. We should try to include her more in our activities. Brynne's eyes carry the weight of loneliness that no one should feel.

After I make their drinks, I start to clean up, locking the doors when seven hits.

"Oh gosh, we should go." Brynne starts to stand.

"No, please don't. It's nice to have company when I'm cleaning up. Besides, I live closer to you than Adeline does. I can drive you home," I insist.

Adeline catches my gaze and nods.

The kitchen is already clean, so I go through my closing routine out front, chatting with them as I work.

"How is it going with Young Jae?" Adeline asks.

Brynne's eyes widen and she glances away, but I'm pretty sure I catch her grinning.

"Good. I felt terrible this morning, I accidentally woke him up, and if I know anything about Young Jae, it's that he doesn't get out of bed a minute before seven, and that's still early." Giggling, I shrug. "He was a good sport about it. Though I won't be surprised if he's asleep when I get home."

Adeline leans back in her chair. "You know, you are calling it home, but I think I only heard you call Jake's place home maybe twice in the year I've known you."

Avoiding her gaze, I clear the dishes from their table. "I didn't realize."

She bites back a grin, standing to stop me. "I've got these. Finish up in here."

Brynne moves to help me lift chairs off the floor so I can sweep and mop. "It's nice to see you smiling again like you used to."

Her comment gives me pause.

"I'm sorry, I shouldn't have overstepped." She backtracks, her cheeks vibrant.

Shaking my head, I hold her gaze. "No need to apologize. I just didn't realize my unhappiness was so obvious."

She licks her lips, her shoulder scrunched up a bit. "I'm an obsessive observer of people. I can usually tell how people in this town are simply by looking at them. I doubt it was obvious to anyone else."

"Ah, yeah. I'm happy now. I'm not supposed to dread going home, and I finally don't." We finish picking up the chairs and she offers to mop after I sweep.

By the time we finish, I'm shutting the lights off a good forty-five minutes earlier than usual.

We say goodbye to Adeline and get into my car.

"I'm in Poplar Grove." Brynne buckles herself in.

"Okay." I pull out of the parking lot and head toward her place. We're quiet, but it doesn't feel weird. It's nice.

Brynne's apartment is in the oldest part of town. It's one of the few buildings that hasn't been upgraded in the past few years and the wear is obvious.

"Thanks for the ride. I could've walked." Brynne shifts, uncomfortable at accepting help.

"It was no problem at all," I reply, my voice emphatic.

She doesn't move to get out of the car. "I meant what I said. I'm happy to see you happy. You deserve it."

She doesn't wait for my response, letting herself out of my car and shutting the door with a wave.

Smiling as I drive to Young Jae's, Brynne's brusqueness takes me back to the times I would talk to her at school. She wouldn't say much and held herself at a distance, but by the time we graduated there was a grudging friendship.

I'm sad it faded away, but seeing her tonight reminds me that it's never too late.

I park on my side of the driveway, a knot forming in the pit of my stomach. Turning up the music, I sit through a couple songs just like I used to. What if I walk in there, and it's exactly the same as at Jake's?

Shaking my head, I mutter, "Young Jae would never."

As the song ends, I turn off my car and grab my purse. The door is unlocked, so I let myself in.

Kimchi greets me at the door, her scruffy body wriggling in excitement. I laugh, greeting her as I put my shoes away. And only my shoes. I pop into the garage to put the cannolis into the spare fridge Young Jae keeps there, that way I can surprise him later.

Wandering toward the kitchen, I smell something delicious and the anxious pit in my stomach unravels. I don't make it past the dining area, my stomach grumbling. The table has a covered dish on it and a huge bowl of rice. Everything is set and ready for us to eat.

"Perfect timing! I just finished cooking." He sits down, waiting while I quickly wash my hands in the bathroom before he starts dishing up. As I take my seat, he says, "I hope you don't mind, I was craving kimchi jjigae."

Breathing in deeply as he takes the lid off the serving dish, I sigh in anticipation. "You know this is one of my favorites. Thank you for cooking dinner."

Serving myself, I take the first bite and it's just as good as I remember.

"It's nice and easy after a long day." Young Jae grins, his voice teasing.

"God, I still feel so bad, I know you're not a morning person." Making a mental note to go wide as I leave my room, I give him my best pouty face. "In my defense, the table attacked me."

"So you said." He laughs. "It's all good. I got more done this morning than I usually do in a day."

We finish eating, laughing and chatting. I shoo him to the living room when he tries to clear the table. "What did I say about cleaning up when you cook?"

"Okay, okay. You win."

Stacking the empty dishes, I mentally prepare myself for the kitchen. I avoided looking at it when I saw the table so I could enjoy my meal, but as I turn and see the clear counters, I falter. Not only are there no dishes, but everything has been wiped down.

I load the dishwasher and see it's ready to run, so I turn it on before joining Young Jae in the living room. "You didn't have to clean the kitchen."

He's lounging on the couch, Kimchi on his lap, as he picks up some spy novel. "I always clean as I cook, I hate eating with a dirty kitchen. Besides, it's my routine and I'm not going to change it just because I know you'll pick up my slack."

His tone is a bit pointed. I feel guilty and know my reaction could be interpreted as comparing him to Jake. A huge offense in Young Jae's eyes.

"I know that. Thank yo..." Trailing off as I see the bookshelves on either side of his fireplace. Before they had his novels spread out with a few decorations in between, but now my books fill the shelves beautifully laid out with a bunch of my trinkets from past trips. "Oh my. Did you do this?"

Biting my lower lip, I look up at the ceiling to stop the tears I can feel forming. All of my books are visible, series together and arranged alphabetically by author, just how I like them.

"Well, Ari helped. I couldn't get them to look the way I wanted so I called her." He grimaces. "She said more in the hour she was here than I typically do all day."

Biting back a laugh, I grab the most recent book I was reading and settle into the corner seat of his sectional. "She was probably just thrilled you asked for her help for once."

I can tell by the look on his face I'm right.

"Apparently, Ji Hoon is moving back to town with a buddy. They're re-opening the old auto shop." He doesn't hide the hurt from his voice. "He never mentioned it to me."

Crossing my legs, I lean toward him. "He probably wants to surprise you and Ari didn't realize."

His face clears a bit. "That does sound like something he would do. She didn't mention who he's opening the business with, Mom probably didn't say."

Reaching over, I pat his thigh. "Exactly."

Young Jae relaxes, picking up a paperback from the side table and flipping to a marked page.

Squirming as I try to get comfortable so I can also read, I set my book down and run upstairs to change into my yoga shorts and T-shirt before rejoining Young Jae. Sighing as I sit down, I pick up the book I abandoned and start reading.

As I devour the love story on the pages in front of me, I try to remember the last time I was able to relax after dinner. The house is tidy, and nothing demands my attention. There's no constant background noise of videos and I actually got to enjoy a fulfilling conversation.

Living with Young Jae is going to be a breeze. I know he's in no rush to push me out, which works because, so far, there's nothing in my price range available unless I want to move to Thistle Creek, which isn't convenient for work. So I settle in, happy and content.

Young Jae groans loudly, stretching, causing me to startle. I just got to the scene where they are finally about to admit they're in love too. "Damn, you scared me."

"I can't sit anymore, I'm going to fall asleep. Want to take Kimchi for a walk with me?" The dog jumps up at the word, wriggling and happy.

Closing my book, I shove up from the couch. "Yes, I would love that."

We get Kimchi into her harness and head out. The evening is sunny and the sound of lawn mowers fills the air.

"Ugh. It's like a challenge. Now I need to mow the lawn." Young Jae groans jokingly.

Laughing, I tease, "It's the eternal cycle."

My smile doesn't fade as we walk. My chest feels light and I can feel my shoulders resting lower than they have, the years of tightness easing.

Glancing at Young Jae as he stops to let Kimchi smell a fire hydrant, I'm reminded of our days studying when he first moved here. He always managed to make me smile even on my roughest days. I had the biggest crush on him back then but was too shy to ask him out and figured he wasn't interested when he never made any attempt at flirting.

Now in his thirties, he's still wildly attractive and the fact that he is so considerate enhances it so much more.

My heart flutters a little bit as he crouches down to give Kimchi a treat. *Shit. No.* I locked that down years ago. Every so often I can feel the attraction flare, but the last thing I need is to lust over my best friend.

Looking away, I stretch out my neck.

"Elise?" Young Jae's hand rests on my shoulder, making me jump. The heat of his hand sends shivers through me.

"Yeah?"

"Ready to keep walking?" He looks at me, concerned. "Are you feeling okay? We can turn around."

Clearing my throat, I start walking. "Sorry, I was just thinking how nice it is to spend my evening relaxing."

It's not completely a lie, but there's no effing way I'm about to tell him I was thinking about how attractive he is.

He falls in stride beside me on the outside of the sidewalk. Somehow I never noticed until now that he always does this...and Jake never did.

"Did you set up the help wanted ad?"

"I did. I posted it for only a week. We'll see what my inbox looks like when I go in tomorrow. I did test out chocolate cannolis. There are some in the garage fridge for you." We loop around the neighborhood, waving at neighbors working in their yards as we walk.

"Seriously?! You tell me this now? We're going home for dessert." He starts walking faster, his six-foot-one frame creating distance as I try to keep up.

At only five-foot-five, it's hard to manage. "Hey! I've got shorter legs than you. Your fast walk is a jog for me."

He slows down. "Okay, okay."

"Anyway, I haven't interviewed anyone before, so this will be a new experience." We round the final corner, his house in sight.

"You will do great. I'm proud of you." He bounds up the steps, Kimchi following on his heels, and opens the door. "Now you go get those cannolis and I'll boil water for some tea."

I quickly grab the box and join him at the table, opening the lid and setting it before him.

His eyes widen. "You've never made these before?"

Shaking my head, I grab one and take a bite. "No, but I think it will be nice to add some new things to the menu and remove some others that just aren't as popular as they used to be."

"Good idea. The big chains cycle through a few things, offering only specific items at certain times during the year. Have you considered doing this? It might help create buzz for those items," he says as he takes another one. "This is delicious."

We stay up, polishing off the box before I realize how late it is.

He follows me up the stairs. "I don't know how you wake up that early every day. I'm wiped."

We pause outside our doors. "You get used to it. I will try to be quieter in the morning."

Saying goodnight, I cross the hall to give him a hug. "You've made this transition easy. Thank you, Oppa."

He smiles at the Korean term. "Goodnight, Roomie."

Chapter Five

Elise

The day is quiet, so quiet, I'm positive I could close early and it wouldn't matter. Aside from a few morning regulars, I've only had a handful of customers all day. It's rare that I get through all the next day's prep before closing.

Sighing, I walk around the dining area, adjusting tables and making sure all the surfaces are clean.

When the bell rings, I turn with a wide grin. My smile falls a bit before I catch myself when I see who's there.

Jake stands in the doorway holding a bouquet of flowers. Daisies, one of my least favorite flowers.

Keeping my voice pleasant, I say, "Hi, Jake. Can I get you something?"

"These are for you." He comes closer, pausing when I go behind the counter, but he pastes the smile back on his face and comes as close as he can. "You haven't been replying to my texts."

Planting my hands on the wooden surface, I frown. "There's nothing to say. I'm not moving back in because I know eventually things will go back to how they were."

"You never even gave me a chance." The whiny pitch of his voice grates on my nerves.

Laughing, my brows practically shoot into my hairline. "And that is why I know there is no second chance for us. I spent the better part of three years trying to talk to you about things that needed repair, and nothing changed. The fact that you can't recognize it shows you weren't listening."

He lays the flowers down, reaching over for my hand. "I'm listening now."

"Too late, Jake." Pulling my hand away, I cross my arms, eyes firm on his. I steel my voice as I say, "I'm not interested in getting back together."

Jake opens his mouth to reply when the bell rings again. Young Jae, Owen, and Cameron come in, their laughter cutting out as they take us in. The glares they're directing at Jake are formidable. It's almost comical to see him react.

"We will talk about this later," he murmurs, turning away.

"No, we have nothing left to talk about." My voice is firm, but he doesn't turn around. He skirts around the guys and goes out the door without saying another word.

Grabbing the flowers, I briefly contemplate tossing them in the trash, but it would be a waste. "Do any of you know someone who likes daisies?"

Cam shakes his head. "Nope. And I can't have them at the clinic. They're toxic to animals."

"I don't know anyone either, sorry." Owen comes to the counter, leaning his hip on it. "He's still trying to get you back, hey?"

Rolling my eyes, I nod. "He probably ran out of boxers or clean dishes."

They chuckle before ordering coffee and treats to go.

I wave them off when they go to pay. "On the house. You got him out of here."

Owen nods. "Anytime. Oh, Adeline wants to have you both over for a bonfire on Sunday. Does that work?"

Glancing at Young Jae, he nods.

"Yeah, sounds fun. We will likely be done paddle boarding around six, so let's say seven-thirty?" I pick up the flowers and hand them to Young Jae. "Would you mind giving these to Mrs. Patterson? I think she likes daisies and will likely be in her garden when you get home."

"Sure." He takes the flowers and looks at me. "Everyone who pays attention knows your favorite flowers are dahlias. He should know that if he wants you back."

My heart warms that he remembers how much I love dahlias. I remember telling him in high school and he bought me a bouquet for my birthday that year. And every birthday since.

Smiling at him, I shrug. "It just makes it easier to hold my ground and not feel guilty."

"What time do you think you will be home? I was going to make ramen, I'm feeling lazy." Young Jae lingers as Owen and Cam walk outside with a wave, heads bent together.

"Early. I just need to close up and pack up any leftovers. I want to drop them off at the seniors' home."

He grins, that dimple popping out. "Perfect, let's eat on the couch and watch that reality show you love so much."

"Yes! Sounds like the perfect way to end the day."

That evening, as I come in the door, I bend to greet Kimchi. It's become our little routine over the past four days. I've always wanted a dog and after being greeted so happily every day since moving in, I can't imagine not having one. She follows me in and when I see a fresh vase of dahlias on the dining table, I pause.

Young Jae glances at me from the couch. "I figured you should get some flowers you will actually enjoy."

Smiling, I bend to smell them. "I love them. Before we settle in, I'm going to change real quick."

Bounding up the stairs, I'm in my cozy yoga shorts and T-shirt and back in the living room in less than five minutes. It's my nightly tradition, comfort winning over fashion every time.

I plop next to Young Jae on the couch. "We need to start with season one. It's still the best one."

He clears his throat, leaning forward to grab my bowl of ramen and handing it to me. Our fingers brush and it's hard to ignore the flutter in my stomach. It feels like more than friends and roommates coming home to flowers and dinner ready. A cozy night on the couch together.

Shoving that aside, I explain the premise of the show as he finds it and hits play.

"They're trying to gain popularity to get special privileges. The one who is the most influential wins the money at the end." My hands wave as the first contestant is introduced. My eyes rapt on the screen as I dig into the ramen.

By the time we've finished eating, he's hooked.

"Okay, I can admit this is entertaining." He chuckles as I dance in the spot, gloating that I knew he'd like it.

Standing, I stretch. "I will clear the dishes, and then I have some treats for us."

I clean up while he watches, rejoining him with cinnamon buns.

"This works out. You come home to dinner and I get dessert." He takes a bite, closing his eyes as he chews. Heat runs through me as his Adam's apple bobs and he swallows with an appreciative moan.

Damn, what is happening? I haven't reacted like this to Young Jae since my mid-twenties.

Stretching my neck, I nibble at my own bun. Granted, we haven't spent this much time together in a long time. And when I was with Jake, I ensured that our boundaries were healthy and our relationship was nothing that could cause question. I just never expected these feelings of attraction to pop up again.

But I've managed it before, I know I can again. I just need to ensure I don't let him know there are feelings deeper than friendship. The last thing I want to do is jeopardize our relationship.

Chapter Six

Young Jae

Elise hops out of the car, grabbing the pie she made earlier before leading the way to Adeline's door.

Our outing today felt different—there was no limit on the time we spent together, and it felt weird going home with her instead of parting ways. I'm not sure what's changing, but it's leaving me unsettled.

The door opens, and Adeline greets us. "Come on in! Dinner is just about ready."

Her two huge dogs, Kane and Stella, sit at attention behind her. I scratch their heads as we pass, following her through the house.

The home is beautiful, a testament to the hard work she and Owen did last year. My lips twitch when I think about how much he used to complain about her and here they are in love and living together.

"I hope you don't mind we kept it simple. Steak, twice baked potatoes, and Greek salad." Adeline grabs wine glasses as Owen comes up from the basement with a bottle of wine. "We thought we would eat outside. It's such a beautiful evening."

"Sounds delicious. I brought peach pie for dessert." We follow them outside, Adeline's deck is a work of art. It's two-tiered and set up for entertaining.

A fire is lit in the firepit and candles glow from lanterns all around the deck. We head to the table under the pergola, where the food is laid out under covers, and even more candles are lit.

It all feels very date-like, especially with the unsubtle glances exchanged between Adeline and Owen as they sit on the same side of the table. Their transparent attempt at matchmaking is comical, but little do they know that Elise doesn't feel that way about me.

I ignore the rush I get when I pull the seat out for Elise, the way she accidentally brushes against me as she goes to sit. Maybe I've been single for too long, I've noticed these feelings coming up a lot in the past year, and I chalked it up to just appreciation for her, but the heat is growing harder to ignore.

Sitting beside her, I gratefully accept a glass of wine and take a sip, my thoughts chaotic, as Adeline and Elise talk about some upcoming girls' trip.

Elise has always been the woman where the timing isn't right and by now we've established too much of a friendship to risk, but part of me seems to be forgetting that. It has been a while since I've had any sort of meaningful connection. My heart is just getting confused with having her around so much more and in more intimate spaces.

That doesn't explain the masquerade ball. The little voice in my head taunts. That night was something else. Holding her in my arms as we danced. It felt right, like home.

Taking a sip of wine, I shove my thoughts into the Elise box and focus on the meal and my friends.

"How are you feeling now that it's been a week since you moved out of Jake's and in with Young Jae?" Adeline asks as she cuts her steak.

Elise smiles, her fingers playing with the stem of her wine glass. "I'm happy. I didn't realize just how much anxiety I had going home and how much of my limited free time I spent cleaning up after Jake."

She looks at me, her expression warm. "You're a very considerate roommate."

Grinning, I look at our friends. "I have to admit, I am knocking it out of the park. Considering I've never lived with anyone except my family before."

They laugh and Elise tells them about how I surprised her by getting her books set up and how much she enjoys having Kimchi to snuggle.

"I feel bad though, because I know I wake you up almost every morning, no matter how quiet I try to be." She looks at me, the guilt clear on her face.

Shaking my head, I lie, "Nah, you're good."

The reality is, she does. I'm not used to having the extra noise in my house and Kimchi scratches on my door after she leaves. Most mornings I'm able to fall back asleep, but it's definitely been a growing pain.

After dinner, we move to the fire, pie in hand.

By the time we leave, Elise is yawning and I'm grateful tomorrow is her day off. We both need a good night's sleep.

***

Eyeing my phone, I pick it up and call my mom. I haven't had a chance to talk to her about retiring. Actually if I'm being honest, I've been avoiding it.

"Young Jae? Gwaenchana?" She asks if I'm okay since I rarely call her during the workday.

"Gwaenchana. I just had a moment before a meeting and realized I haven't checked in for a while. How are you and Appa doing?" I ease in, hoping to butter her up.

"Busy. Things at the inn are steady, which is good. Otherwise, everything is the same. Jamsiman." She covers the mouthpiece and starts talking rapidly. I'm assuming to Appa based on what little I pick up.

When she comes back on the line, I finally bite the bullet. "Have you and Appa thought about slowing down? I think it would be nice for the two of you to spend time relaxing. Besides, Ari has her business management degree. She's ready to step up."

Silence. That's all that comes over the phone before she starts ranting at me.

"Relax? Why would I need to relax? Ari hasn't been running this inn for fifteen years. She's been full-time for two. She's not ready." Her voice is sharp, that unbending tone she's always had.

"Eomma, that's not fair to Ari. She's been working at the inn just as long as you in some capacity. She is ready and she doesn't need ten more years of being sidelined to do a good job. Her ideas are good—"

"Aigoo. My children. No appreciation for the hard work we've done. We will retire when it's time. I don't want to hear of it again." She hangs up, leaving me slack-jawed.

Ari was right. Talking to her about retirement is like stepping on a land mine. Kaboom.

I leash Kimchi to walk her before my meeting, checking my phone as it starts buzzing with texts from Ari.

I'm sorry, Oppa. I really thought she might be more receptive.

Chuckling, I type back.

She will come around. We can try again another day, maybe six months down the road.

She sends an exasperated GIF back. Smirking, I finish my walk and head home for an afternoon of meetings.

***

Shutting down my laptop, I lean back in my chair. Kimchi takes it as an invitation to sit on my lap.

"Well, damn." I scratch her ears, still amazed at how that meeting went.

My office door cracks open, Elise peeking in with a fresh pot of coffee in hand. "Well damn, what?"

"That was the head of municipal development for Thistle Creek. They are restoring the grain elevator and want me to design the inside. They're going to turn it into a museum, art gallery, and library all in one." I can barely contain the excitement in my voice. These are the projects I live for.

I hold out my mug, grateful for a top up.

"Incredible." She holds her hand up for a high-five, which I give her. "I've never been to Thistle Creek. If you want company on a scouting mission, I am happy to go with you."

Leaning back in my chair, I grin. "I do need to head out there. It can wait until next Monday, so let's go then. We can make a day of it."

She sets the coffee pot on my desk, scoops Kimchi out of my lap, and dances around with her. "It's a plan."

We laugh as the dog wriggles out of Elise's arms onto the floor, crouching down and wagging her stumpy tail.

Her excited wriggle turns into barking when the doorbell rings.

"You answer the door, and I will put the coffee away." Standing, I head to the kitchen with the dishes I accumulated during the day and start tidying up.

Elise lets out an excited scream and Kimchi starts barking even more. Rushing to the front door, I halt when I see her throwing herself into the arms of my older brother.

It's been about nine months since I last saw him and he looks exactly the same, maybe a bit more tired.

Despite being four years older than me, some days I feel like the more grounded one.

His eyes dance with humor as he looks up at me. My body feels tight as he hugs Elise and swings her around. He smirks at me as he sets her down, tucking her into his side.

Striding over, I resist the urge to pull her out of his arms. "This is a surprise."

His brows raise, his grin knowing as he releases Elise from his grasp. "A good one I hope."

I can't stop the smile as I hug my brother. "Always."

"Come in! Come in!" Elise moves back, scooping Kimchi into her arms and making her way to the kitchen. "There's some fresh coffee in the pot. Do you still like it black?"

Ji Hoon calls out an affirmative before turning to me and lowering his voice. "There's lots you haven't been telling me."

Shutting the door as he comes in, I glare at him. "You're one to talk. I had to hear through Ari that you're moving back. And endure her gloating about it."

"I wanted to surprise you." He points down the hall, where we can hear Elise talking to Kimchi. "Elise is here looking pretty cozy, and you have a dog!"

He follows me into the living room as Elise joins us, handing my brother a mug of coffee.

"Her name is Kimchi, and he kept her from me too." She winks at me.

"For like two hours." My protest is buried as Elise sits between me and Ji Hoon, continuing their conversation as though I'm not there.

"And Young Jae is kindly letting me stay here while I look for a place." She crosses her legs, leaning back into the couch. "My ex-boyfriend was kind of a dud. And I finally had enough. But you know how Willowbrook Lake is. It's not abundant in its rental housing."

Ji Hoon laughs. "Do I ever. I'm staying with Eomma and Appa. It's why Liam isn't here yet. He's wrapping some things up while I find us a place."

"If you're buying, Raelynn is a real estate agent. She's down to part-time but is still amazing," Elise suggests.

He hums. "Yeah, maybe. I was able to save a good amount of money and we borrowed what we need for the auto shop. What do you think of the name *Wheel Be All Right*?"

She laughs. "I love it."

"I agree, it's clever," I chime in.

"Construction on the shop starts in a month, until then I just need to keep Mom and Dad off my back about finding a wife." Ji Hoon cringes. "Mom asked if Liam and I are more than friends and said it was okay. Very progressive of her, but super awkward."

We laugh. My parents want happiness for all of us, but I know they wish we would all settle down. I fear they're going to add more pressure on Ari, being the youngest.

"What made you move back here to set up shop?" Elise asks, stifling a yawn.

"We know that Willowbrook Lake prefers locally owned shops to franchises, and there hasn't been a functioning mechanic shop in town for close to eight years. When Liam and I decided to open our own instead of working for someone else, we thought we'd have a better chance here. Fill a gap where it's needed. And I wanted to be close to family again. Besides, Liam is tired of living in the city. He has his own reasons. It just worked out." His passion is obvious when he talks about it, but what sticks out most is the sense of sadness when talking about being close to family again.

I had no idea he was having a hard time being away from us.

"Well, I know we're all thrilled to have you close to home again." I'm emphatic, trying to show how much I missed him without getting too sappy.

One side of his lips tilt up, the smallest hint of gratitude.

As we chat, Elise dozes off. Kimchi snuggled into the curve of her stomach. Standing, I grab a blanket and cover her.

"So, how is it living with the woman you've been pining for the last decade and a half?" He smirks at me.

"I haven't been pining for her," I grumble.

Ji Hoon scoffs. "Sure. And I won't be a bachelor forever."

Sighing, I glance at her. "Honestly, it's a little confusing. She walks around in these tiny yoga shorts and oversized T-shirts. It's unexpectedly hot. And it's just nice having her here. I thought those feelings were gone, but I guess I was lying to myself."

He's the one person I would actually talk to about this because Ji Hoon never presses or pushes you in any one direction. It's honestly surprising he hasn't found the one yet and is so determined to stay single, because he would make someone an amazing partner.

"It sounds a little confusing. But I know you will figure it out. The two of you have a special friendship." He claps his hand on my shoulder.

Ji Hoon visits until late. He leaves and I feel like we've finally been able to truly catch up in a way I didn't know I needed.

After locking up and letting Kimchi out to do her business, I ponder her curled up in an awkward position.

"I can't leave her like this," I say to Kimchi, who gives me a judgemental look for even contemplating it. Grabbing her phone from the table, I stuff it in my pocket before bending down, I scoop her into my arms as gingerly as I can. She works harder than most people I know. I haven't pressed about the position she posted, but I do hope she hires someone soon.

She sighs, tucking into me, and my heart leaps. It shouldn't feel this good to have her in my arms.

Steeling myself, I climb the stairs and tuck her into her bed. Kimchi jumps up, curling behind her legs and passing out right along with Elise.

Taking her phone, I plug it into the charger. The screen lights up and I see a message from Jake come in.

Scowling, I put her phone onto do not disturb mode and leave her room. The dude is persistent, but it shouldn't have taken her leaving for him to realize what he had. He never appreciated her and the fact that he isn't respecting her peace now infuriates me.

If he doesn't back off soon, we're going to have a chat.

Chapter Seven

Elise

My second to last interviewee leaves me feeling underwhelmed, just like the previous four. Groaning, I stretch and go make myself a latte. My cell buzzes as I finish, Young Jae's name popping up on the screen.

"Hey." Glancing at the time, I'm relieved I only have one more to go. I can't believe I closed for a half day to conduct interviews and they have been disappointing.

"Uh-oh. You sound exasperated. I take it the interviews aren't going well?" His voice is empathetic.

Sighing, I make my way to the table and pull out the last person's resume. "Three weren't even qualified. The other two met the criteria but didn't read the ad. I just have one more and then I'm done for the day."

"Almost done. And this is only the first round. You can always post the ad again."

I know he's right, but having five back-to-back interviews without even a hint of a potential candidate is discouraging. "True enough."

He chuckles. "I called to tell you I ran into Hank and apparently the planning committee is putting on a last minute picnic at the gazebo. I thought it would be fun to go."

"Really? That's new, but sounds like a fun way to spend some time this evening." The bell rings, my final interview coming in. "My last appointment is here, I gotta go."

We hang up and I stand to greet her.

"Hello, you must be Mary." I extend my hand to shake hers. "I'm Elise Cooper."

"Nice to meet you." Mary's voice is pleasant, and her energy is warm and welcoming. "Thank you for the opportunity to interview."

"I'm glad you were able to make it. Would you like anything to drink? I can whip something up quickly."

She refuses my offer and we settle in. I run through the normal questions about experience and get to know her. Her resume lists some incredible credentials, including running several restaurants.

By the end of the interview, which feels more like a natural conversation, I'm feeling pretty good.

"I'm curious, what made you apply to Perk Up? It's quite different than your previous roles." This question is important. I don't want to be a temporary stop in someone's career journey.

"I'm not ready to retire, but I'm ready to slow down. When I searched Perk Up, the reviews were excellent." She pauses, shrugging her shoulder. "At some point you just want a great place to work. Also my daughter is moving to Thistle Creek. She got hired at the high school teaching English, and this is close but not 'in her hair' close."

Laughing, I nod. "True."

We chat for a bit longer as I expand on what my goals are, and I'm impressed with her engagement in the conversation.

"Well, I don't have anything else I need for now. Do you have any questions for me?" Tucking her info into the file I made, I already know I'm going to offer her the job.

Mary smiles, asking, "I know you have a month from now listed as a start date, but if I'm the successful candidate, would it be possible to start sooner?"

I grin in response. "I'm sure we can work something out."

We say goodbye and I lock up.

"Oh, thank goodness." Relief fills me as I clean up and start prepping for tomorrow. It doesn't take long and I'm amazed at how much quicker things seem to go now that I'm not dreading going home.

When I walk in the door the house is quiet, so I rush upstairs to freshen up and get ready for the picnic at the gazebo. It's a bit random for a Thursday evening, but it's not uncommon for the town to have some impromptu events.

Throwing on a pair of shorts and a flowy tank top, I forgo drying my hair when I hear Young Jae talking to Kimchi. Instead, I quickly throw it in a braid and head downstairs.

Kimchi is sitting on her hind quarters as Young Jae offers her a treat. He's talking to her in Korean. "Yeppoyo." Lips twitching, I listen to him coo about how pretty she is, telling her she's the best dog.

"You are the prettiest dog, Kimchi. He's not lying." I smile when Young Jae jumps, looking a little embarrassed.

"She is." He tosses her the treat before washing his hands and grabbing a small cooler. "I packed some drinks, just in case."

"Shall we walk?" The gazebo is a quick ten-minute walk from Young Jae's, the trail behind his house leading to the lake.

He nods and we head out. "How was your last interview?"

"It was phenomenal. I'm going to offer her the job tomorrow and see when she wants to start. She asked if that was flexible." I gush about the ideas we tossed around and how she wants to be closer to her daughter.

He smiles as I finish. "She sounds perfect. I'm so happy for you." He gently bumps me. "Once she's all trained up, what are you going to do with your free time?"

Scrunching my nose, I think. I don't remember the last time I had a lot of free time. My "free" time is always carefully planned. "Honestly, I have no idea. I should probably find a hobby."

The sun filters through the trees, and the trail is quiet except for some birds tweeting and the sound of our footsteps. Soon we should be able to see the lake through the trees as we close in on the gazebo. It's in a quiet grove of trees just off the lake, leading to a secluded part of the beach.

The town doesn't advertise the space, leaving it primarily for resident use. It's a well-kept secret in the midst of a large and complex trail system.

"You used to enjoy riding. You could always start that again." He suggests, his deep voice low. His arm brushes against mine, making me aware of how closely we're walking together. He's so attentive to me and what I say, genuinely interested in my life. My heart is having a hard time not crossing the line from friendship to more, but the idea of ruining our friendship hurts more than ignoring how everything with him feels right. Easy.

I shrug. "Possibly. I like the idea of not planning it right now. Plus I need to onboard Mary, build the menu, and all that."

We round the bend in the trail, the trees clearing a little as the gazebo comes into view. There is no one there, but there are flickering lights inside.

"What's going on?" My brows pinch together as we close the distance.

Lanterns with candles, blankets spread out, a vase with flowers, and an epic picnic spread fill the center of the gazebo. It looks nothing like a town picnic but more like a date.

"Are you sure this is a town event?" I don't step foot inside, not wanting to ruin someone's hard planning. Peering around us, I don't see or hear anyone.

Young Jae shakes his head. "No, Hank told me that there's a picnic at the gazebo and that we should come..."

We look at each other and then at the sight before us.

Laughing, I creep closer and see even more details. Champagne. Chocolate covered strawberries.

"I'm pretty sure this is a setup." Kicking my shoes off, I sit down. Looking up at him, my laughter falters at the intensity of his gaze. Clearing my throat, I gesture. "Might as well enjoy their hard work. This town does love to meddle, but at least we get a good laugh and meal out of it."

I feel the heat of Young Jae's gaze as he removes his shoes, but I focus on eating a strawberry. My crush is making me see things that aren't there, like attraction.

It's nice. The setting couldn't be better. And I love spending time with Young Jae.

"This does look good." His gaze still on me, he pops a strawberry into his mouth. "If I'm being honest, I'm happy it's just us. I love our town, but you're right, they do love to meddle."

Looking up, I smile at him. "Exactly. The best company and great food."

We really dig in, conversation flowing easily as we eat. Whoever was in on this with Hank outdid themselves. There are little sandwiches and even slices of strawberry rhubarb pie.

It's not until we've polished everything off and Young Jae is carrying the trash to the garbage can that I find the note. It's addressed to me.

It's time to take the leap and trust in the feelings you've been hiding. You never know what might happen.

My heart beats loudly in my ears. If it's so obvious to everyone else, maybe Young Jae knows about my crush too.

Wracking my brain, I try to think of any change in behavior from him, but I can't think of anything that can't be explained away. Tucking it in my pocket as Young Jae comes back to the gazebo, I lean back on my hands and peer out at the lake.

He settles in beside me but faces toward me. The distance between us small, intimate.

"I like seeing you like this. Relaxed and happy." His voice is low, the timbre seductive in a way I don't think he's aware of. When he speaks like that, his accent is more noticeable. "I like having you in my house and seeing you every day."

Sighing in contentment, I murmur, "Back at you."

A breeze blows some loose strands of hair from my braid into my face. Before I can move them away, his hand reaches out and tucks the errant hair behind my ear. The smooth tips of his fingers leave a tingling trail and I shiver in response.

My heart beats faster as he sits up, bringing his face closer to mine. I must be imagining his eyes looking at my lips, but then his fingers stroke along my jaw.

Holding my breath, I can't look away as he leans in, his eyes locked on mine. Heart racing, I pinch my leg. He pauses, his lips mere inches away from mine. Young Jae starts to say something, but his phone rings with Ari's ringtone.

We freeze, but then he backs away and reaches for his cell. Looking away, I take a few deep breaths.

"What, Ari?" His tone is sharp, worried. She only calls if it's something important.

Her voice is loud, but all I can make out is she's talking fast and then he hangs up.

"Ari popped by the house to grab a form for my parents, and Kimchi got out. Ari couldn't catch her and lost sight of her."

Chapter Eight

Young Jae

I can see the panic I'm feeling reflected on Elise's face. We're on our feet and I'm running down the path calling for Kimchi. Elise is on my heels, her voice panicked as she echoes my calls.

Stopping where the path forks to go behind my house or to the front, I try to breathe and think.

Where would Kimchi go?

Elise stops next to me, her hands on her knees as she pants. Her brows are pinched together and I can see the strain around her eyes.

Reaching out, I cup her cheek and try to remain calm. It hasn't been that long since Kimchi got out. "We will find her."

She nods. "You go that way and I will check the front."

Before I can respond, she's hurrying away, calling Kimchi, her voice thick and frantic. I slow down a bit, trying to search with more thought, whistling and calling the dog just like I do when she's in the yard. I reach where my house backs to the trail and peek over the fence just to make sure.

Turning, I call Kimchi again when a white blur emerges from the bushes opposite the trail from my house. My knees buckle as she jumps into my arms, her tongue draped out of the side of her mouth as she wiggles happily.

Hugging her close, I exhale heavily. "You gave us a damn heart attack."

Standing, I adjust my grip on Kimchi so she's comfortable and rush toward where I can hear Elise calling, her voice getting more frightened.

Coming out of the pathways, I follow Elise's voice until I find her coming out of a cul-de-sac up the road.

She turns to go further, so I holler, "Elise, I found her."

Elise whips around and runs to us. I can see tear tracks running down her cheeks. She throws her arms around me and Kimchi, burying her face into Kimchi's fur. She's mumbling, but I can't make out the words.

"She was in the bushes behind my house." My nerves settle as I hand Kimchi to Elise, watching her snuggle and chastise the dog for running out the door.

Now that the haze of fear is clearing, that moment in the gazebo flashes back. Was I seriously about to kiss my best friend?

And was it me, or was she leaning in as well?

Glancing away, I scoff silently. She was probably thinking I was getting some chocolate off her face or leaning in to tell her something. Living with her, seeing her completely at ease all the time and in different situations than normal, it's messing with me. And those shorts and T-shirts she lounges in all day don't help anything. She's so effortlessly sexy.

And the picnic. How did Hank get wrangled into that?

The town needs to stop meddling where they don't belong.

***

Elise greets me Monday morning with a basket of goodies and freshly brewed coffee. Her long hair is pulled up into a ponytail and she's wearing a pink summer dress that hugs her curves before flowing loosely from her hips. It kills me.

"How long do you think we're staying in Thistle Creek?" Laughing, I lift the basket, groaning and slumping to the side.

She laughs, sauntering past me with the coffee, her dress swaying with her hips. "I figured we could make it a day trip. I've never been to Thistle Creek and we might as well go see the gnomes in Mistik Ridge as well."

I follow her to the car, getting in before I turn to gape at her. "Gnomes? I've never heard of these gnomes, and I've been to Mistik Ridge a few times. I was in a small-town business owner group with the woman who owns the inn, Tasha, and we met frequently there until about five years ago."

She chuckles. "It's a cute story. It's a love story between two of the townspeople. She was a tenant in his house, and they didn't click because he was a bit uptight. So she ordered these vulgar gnomes to drive him nuts. Long story short, they're in love and now these gnomes are spread throughout the town in all their vulgar glory. It's a huge tourist attraction, and they even posted about it on their website. We have to go see these gnomes."

"We can make the trip. Why don't we stop by the inn for lunch?" It's been a while since I saw it. I'm sure Tasha is doing amazing things with it.

Elise smiles, her excitement palpable.

The drive passes quickly as we sing songs from the '90s playlist we made together a few years ago. When we get to Thistle Creek, Elise turns the volume down, peering around her. It's quaint. A little bigger than Willowbrook Creek, but it doesn't feel that way.

I pull into the parking lot for the grain elevator and see a few people waiting.

"Did you want to take my car and explore?" I hold out the keys.

Elise shakes her head. "Is it okay if I join you? I'm happy to take notes. I'd love to see the process for this."

Nodding, I don't say much as we get out of the car. I love that she wants to learn about what I do and see a project that is the culmination of everything I got into architecture for.

The building is amazing and in excellent condition considering how old it is. It still maintains its structural integrity, a thorough report was done with a structural engineer.

Elise takes notes and collects any of the needed documents the committee has put together for me.

"I think we should build mezzanines that we stagger so we can still see the entire space." Gesturing as I go over each area they had highlighted, I point out how we can incorporate the history of the building into the redevelopment.

As we wrap up, Elise and I linger in the building.

"This place is going to be incredible. The way you describe your vision for it, I'm in awe," Elise gushes as she hands me everything she's holding, which she's organized into a neat stack.

"Just wait until I show you my renderings, I'm itching to get started."

We head back outside, hit by a wall of heat.

"Let's walk a bit, explore," she suggests.

A path around the grain elevator leads right to the creek. It's bigger than I expected, and the water flows steadily through town. We meander down the path before finding a little dock.

Elise kicks off her shoes before sitting on the edge and dangling her feet into the water. Sitting beside her, I sigh as the cool water runs over my skin.

Glancing at her in my peripheral, she seems lost in thought. I can't help but wonder if she's thinking about the almost kiss. We never talked about it, returning to normal as though it never happened. However, it still lingers in the air whenever I'm near her, my mind automatically going down the "what if" path.

I wonder if she would have kissed me back or if she would have pushed me away.

And is she not saying anything because she wants to pretend it never happened and go back to the way things were, or is she waiting for me to broach the subject since I'm the one who leaned in? It's hard to feel so deeply for the person I consider to be one of my best friends but it's impossible to ignore my feelings when I'm around her all the time.

She hums. "It's a beautiful day. I like the creek, but nothing beats the lake at home."

Agreeing, I glance at the time. "Why don't we explore town a bit and then head to Mistik Creek for lunch?"

"Lunch and then gnomes."

Laughing, I stand before offering my hand to help her up. She stumbles a bit, and I catch her, holding on for a moment before I drop my arms. When she looks up at me, her expression almost has me finishing what I tried to start. Instead, I grin and tease, "Easy, if you fall in the creek, I don't have a towel or an extra shirt today."

She scrunches her nose at me playfully, reminded of the day when she fell into the lake before she slips her feet back into her sandals.

We wander Thistle Creek for an hour, looking in some kitschy stores. Elise buys some water paintings done by a local artist before we head back to my vehicle and we make the short thirty minute drive to Mistik Ridge.

My stomach growls loudly as I turn onto the inn's long driveway. When Elise giggles, the sound goes straight to my gut and, even worse, to my dick as well. The soft scent of her perfume has filled my car, so I'm surrounded by her.

We park by the veranda, my eyes taking in the chipped paint. As I look over the entire building, I see how run-down it is. I remember it was a fixer-upper when she bought it, but it's been years, and in my mind, it was a bustling, beautiful inn.

Tasha appears on the porch, her brows pinched until I get out of the car, walking around to open Elise's door.

"Oh my goodness! Young Jae?" Tash bounds down the steps, her friendly smile almost hiding the stress around her eyes.

She gives me a quick hug before turning to Elise and introducing herself.

"It's been a long time." She gushes at me before ushering us into the building. "What did I do to earn this visit?"

"Elise wanted to see the gnomes, so we thought we'd pop in for lunch. I hope that's okay." The inside shows wear, but you can tell that she has been working hard to maintain it.

Her expression shifts for the briefest moment before her smile is back. "Of course. Come in, come in. I wasn't expecting anyone today, so I hope you're okay with something simple."

We agree, following her into the kitchen.

Elise catches my eyes, her expression confused and worried.

"Things have been a bit tough since I bought the place. The inspector missed a bunch of big things, and the expenses have piled up. I've had to consider bringing on a partner." This time she lets her sadness show a moment, before she straightens her shoulders. "No matter. No mountain is too high, right?"

She whips up chicken salad sandwiches on fresh croissants, with fresh lemonade and no bake cheesecake. It's delicious and Elise asks for her recipe.

We catch up, Tash filling us in on bringing on a new partner. She tries to keep her voice perky, but I can tell she's not happy about it. There's a fire in her eyes that I remember from when we first met.

"If you need anything for designs, let me know. And I have a friend who does a lot of contract work. He is reasonable and does amazing work." I hand her Owen's card, hoping I'm not overstepping.

"Thank you, this is—amazing. And I'm so glad I got to meet you, Elise." She looks between us, her expression wistful. "You're a cute couple. I'm glad you found someone so wonderful. You deserve it."

Before Elise can say anything, I simply thank her and we head out. I'm curious if I will hear about it in the car, but as we turn to head toward town, she's looking at me, her eyes wide. "We need to help her. Did you see the look on her face when she was talking about this new partner? It's killing her to do that."

Humming, I rub my jaw as I drive the short distance to town and these gnomes. "Possibly, she looked more determined than anything. It might not be a bad thing. Sometimes we need that push to light our fire."

We park along the main street in town. Just like home and Thistle Creek, it's quaint and well-kept.

As we get out of the car, the first gnome is in a flowerpot on the sidewalk. The gnome looks to be passed out, and his pants are around his knees.

Elise bursts out laughing and takes a photo.

We walk along the street toward the community info center, where a brochure boasts a scavenger hunt of the gnomes. Advertising seasonal changes.

Shaking my head, I grab the pamphlet and we start to hunt.

As we find more, checking them off, I chuckle. "I have to admit, this is brilliant. I want to come back in the fall to see the new gnomes and find them in the new locations."

"Maybe we could make it a group activity?" Elise replies as she takes a sharp left into a neighborhood.

We hunt for close to two hours before finding all the gnomes. By the time we get home, I realize that my heart won't let me ignore the way I feel about Elise, but I don't know what to do about it.

Chapter Nine

Elise

The next several weeks fly by. Mary starts at Perk Up and picks up quickly on all the normal tasks. Her insight into possible menu items is well-thought out and by the end of July Perk Up is offering a variety of hot food items.

I love having someone to work with in the afternoons, and the shop has been bustling as I roll out the changes. The town loves Mary almost as much as I do. She reminds me of my mom, the little I remember her.

Young Jae and I have fallen into a comfortable routine. I sneak out in the morning and he pretends to sleep through it. After I'm done working, I come home to dinner and then we go for a walk. Every Sunday we spend the afternoon together and I can't remember the last time I've been this happy.

He hasn't mentioned the moment we shared at the gazebo or attempted to make any moves. Sometimes I think I misread the situation, but then there are moments when he will brush the hair off my neck, or I catch him looking at my lips.

It's becoming harder every day to keep my thoughts away from Young Jae and that moment. I wish I could talk about it with my friends, but I don't know if

I'm ready to hear what they have to say, mostly because I know exactly what it will be.

"*Why don't you go for it?*"

"*You know there's more there.*"

I've heard it before.

"That was a heavy sigh," Mary prods gently. "I know that sigh. Whenever Morgan makes that sound, it means man trouble. Want to talk about it?"

Propping myself against the counter, I tap my fingers against the wood. I haven't talked to Adeline or Rae about this, they would encourage me to make a move and I just can't be the one to cross the boundary. I don't know what's holding me back, maybe the idea of my best friend rejecting me in the gentle way I know he would and the damage that would do to our friendship—I just don't think my heart could recover.

Taking a deep breath, I huff out the air and nod. "You know Young Jae?"

She smiles, the lines around her eyes creasing. "That handsome young man who comes in here all the time? I'm familiar."

"Well, we've been friends for ages, but I've had a crush on him since we met. I was fooling myself thinking it went away, but now that we live together, I realize I was just ignoring it." Standing, I pace along the cabinet of treats, tidying. "Living with him has been wonderful and if anything, I think my heart is even more attached."

Her gaze turns knowing. "You're in love with him."

"I think maybe I always have been. But I don't think he feels the same, or maybe he does a little but not enough to take a chance." I shrug. "I don't know what to do."

She hums. "I can see the predicament, but if I've learned anything, these things tend to come to a head at some point. You can decide if you want to lead the charge or if you want to wait and see."

The bell jingles and we both turn. Jake walks in with more daisies. Groaning, I roll my eyes at Mary.

He has persistently brought me flowers every week despite me telling him to stop.

"Hey, Elise. Mary." He greets us. I can see the sadness when he looks at me and feel bad.

"Jake," I sigh.

"I know, but I'm not giving up." He sets the flowers down, his eyes earnest. "Just a meal. Just one, and if you still feel like there's nothing to salvage, then I will stop."

Groaning, I pick up the daisies and hand them back to him. "Fine. One meal. But stop bringing me daisies. I don't like them and they're toxic to dogs, so I can't even bring them home."

His face flickers with surprise, lips turning down a little. It was always a source of contention when we were together. I wanted a dog, he said they were too much work, despite me being the one who cleaned the house.

Jake shakes off whatever is going through his head and grins, elated, taking the flowers back. "I will pick you up tonight at six."

***

"You're going to dinner with Jake? How the hell did that happen?" Young Jae glowers as he sits on the edge of the tub in my bathroom while I get ready for dinner. Jake should be here in fifteen minutes, and I finally told Young Jae that I had agreed to go to dinner with him.

Sighing, I meet his gaze through the mirror. "He isn't letting up and he said if we go out for dinner and I still don't want to give him another chance, he will quit coming around. So, I agreed. It's one meal that will ultimately close out that chapter for good."

Picking up my lipstick, I return to getting ready.

"Why are you putting on lipstick to turn him down?" Young Jae grumbles.

Biting back a smile, I apply the neutral color. If I didn't know better, I'd think he was jealous.

Finishing up, I head back into my bedroom with him trailing behind. Kimchi is chewing on a toy on my bed. He plops down beside her and starts playing tug-of-war with her as I go into my closet. I change quickly before rejoining them.

He looks up and shakes his head. "Nope. You look way too hot for a closure date. He's not going to stop if you show up looking like that."

Biting back a grin, I roll my eyes. "You're exaggerating. I've worn this a ton. It's not like it's special."

Standing in front of my mirror, I look at the floor length maxi-dress. It's floral with a subtle V-neck. Not too revealing, but perfect for summer.

Before he can come back with anything, the doorbell rings. Kimchi takes off, barking as she runs to the door. I grab my purse, Young Jae following closely behind.

I open the door to Jake standing there with a bouquet of roses. Better than daisies but still nowhere near my top five favorite flowers. At least I can have these in the house.

Kimchi rushes out to greet him, he stares down but doesn't greet her. I know he's not an animal person, but it rubs me the wrong way that he doesn't even say hi. It's another confirmation that he's not right for me and I was settling when I was trying to make it work.

"Hey. You look beautiful." Jake looks relieved as Kimchi runs back in the house to sit next to a watchful Young Jae.

"Thanks." I start to slip into my shoes, Jake opening the door wider.

He opens his mouth to say something, faltering as Young Jae comes to stand next to me, wrapping his arm around my shoulders. "She does, not that you deserve it. If you're trying to win her back, remembering that dahlias are her favorite flower would be a good start. Who am I kidding? You never cared about her enough to actually learn her favorites."

Jake's mouth opens and closes, his face flushed. His embarrassment is clear and he has the wherewithal to look a little ashamed.

"It's too late though. You're not going to win her back because she knows how good life can be now. So don't keep her out too late. Remember, we have plans tonight."

Taking in the scene before me, I realize I need to put a stop to all this.

"Jake, saying yes to dinner was a bad idea. I'm sorry, but you should just go," I say and close the front door.

Suppressing a giggle, I gasp when Young Jae kisses me. His lips moving over mine, his tongue delving deeper.

My heart pounds as I drop my purse, my arms wrapping around his neck on their own volition as I kiss him back. My entire body tingles, electricity thrumming through me as I press into him. We kiss until the noise of a revving motor sounds.

Pulling away, I lick my lips and glance over to Young Jae. My heart pounds as I finally meet his gaze.

Young Jae smiles at me. "Well, that took care of that! You don't have to suffer through a dinner with him and he definitely won't be around again."

Clearing my throat, my heart sinks into my chest. "Um, yeah. Thanks for that."

I follow him into the house, my body still wired from the kiss.

"Since you're all dressed up, why don't we go for dinner?" He turns so suddenly I crash into him. His hands automatically grab my waist, holding me steady.

Staring up at him, all thoughts leave my head as he licks his lips.

"Elise?"

"Hmm?" My eyes linger on his lips until they start twitching. Lifting my eyes, I hold his gaze, his brown eyes intense on mine. He smells so good, I'm in a fog until he grins cocking his head slightly. I finally process his question. "Oh, dinner. Yeah. Sounds good."

The drive to Cliff's helps clear my head as Young Jae talks about the progress on the grain elevator development. His passion as he elaborates on the progress pushes thoughts about the kiss aside, but I still send Adeline and Rae a "what the fuck" message.

The parking lot at Cliff's is packed. "If we want the town to stop meddling, we may want to go home."

Young Jae just laughs, getting out of the vehicle. "We've eaten together before."

There are people waiting to be seated when we get inside, but as soon as Cara, the hostess, sees us, she waves us over.

"We have a table ready for you." She ushers us to the back corner where all the private booths are.

Confused, we follow her. "We didn't book anything," Young Jae mentions as we weave through the crowded bar.

Cara just smiles and takes us to the final booth. It's intimate and quiet compared to the rest of the bar. I've never sat in this area, but it's a newer addition that Cliff added, wanting to give couples a quieter, more romantic space.

The table has a bouquet of dahlias and a lantern lit in the center. The rest of the lights dimmed.

She leaves with a promise to return with water and we sit in the intimate booth. It's small, ensuring we need to sit next to each other.

"Did you?" I ask.

Young Jae shakes his head, looking as confused as I feel. "No. And I didn't tell anyone we were coming here."

"Oh my god. I did. I told Adeline and Rae." Laughing, I look at Young Jae. The candlelight dances across his face and the words on my lips fall away. He looks so good and his lips still have a hint of my lipstick from earlier.

Young Jae's lips twitch. "They must've called. Well, we were going to eat dinner anyway, and it is nice and quiet back here."

He drapes his arm over the back of the cushion, the weight of it against my upper back.

Cara returns with water and two glasses of wine. "Wine's on the house." She winks again, leaving us to decide what to eat.

Chapter Ten

Young Jae

Kissing Elise was even better than I imagined it would be and her response told me everything I needed to know. The way she leaned into me, her body practically melting into mine. The feel of her lips responding eagerly, her arms around my neck. My feelings aren't unreciprocated at all. The guise of rescuing her from Jake the perfect excuse and now nothing will hold me back.

We eat dinner, conversation flowing smoothly as always, and if it wasn't for the lingering glances, the way she's leaned into me a little as our evening progresses, I would think I'd misread her response. But I know what I felt and I know I'd be a fool to think there was no feeling in her response.

After dinner, Cara brings dessert. A slice of mocha cheesecake with two forks. Elise digs in, a soft moan escaping as she scoops a forkful and holds it up for me.

"This is the best cheesecake I've ever had."

Leaning in, I hold her gaze as I take her fork into my mouth, an explosion of flavor hitting my tongue.

We alternate bites until it's gone, Elise setting the fork down and leaning back into the booth, her head dropping onto my shoulder. She sighs, patting her flat stomach. "I'm so full, that was incredible."

Her voice is full of contentment, soft and hitting me right in the gut.

She rolls her head to look at me. "I'm so glad we're here together."

Staring into her green eyes, I brush a strand of hair away before dropping my hand away. "Me too."

The air between us thickens, I don't notice Cara until she clears her throat. "Your bill has been taken care of, but stay as long as you like."

Her lips curl into a smirk as she leaves, wishing us a good night.

"That was nice of someone," Elise murmurs, her eyes bright as she watches me.

"It was, but let's head out. No need to give the town more to talk about," I reply, sliding out of the booth.

Our drive home is charged. We don't say much, but as we get closer to home, Elise starts shifting in her seat more. I catch her gaze a couple times, my dick hardening when I see the heat in her expression.

Pulling into the garage, I lurch to a stop beside her car. I yank my key out of the ignition and am out of the car before she's even unbuckled. Opening the door for her, my entire body feels electric as she brushes past me. The bang of her car door is loud in the silence of the garage as I follow her into the house.

Her movements are methodical as she hangs her bag up and puts away her shoes. Maybe I misread the energy in the car. I put my shoes away.

As I straighten, she's suddenly in my arms, her lips on mine.

Groaning, I grab her hips and lift. The fabric of her dress bunches around her hips as I pull her into me. Elise moans softly as she presses against my erection. Her tongue strokes mine as she grinds her hips, her fingers running through my hair.

The fog of arousal in my head clears enough that I start moving. Elise moves her lips to my jaw and down my neck, pressing herself as close as she possibly can.

My body is thrumming as I kick my bedroom door shut, crawling onto my king-sized bed, laying her down. Her hair fans around her. Her lips curve into a sultry smile, eyes heavy with arousal.

Capturing her lips with mine, I press into her. Kissing Elise, having her beneath me, is beyond my mediocre fantasies. The way she smells, her eager responses. The quickening of her breath. Everything about her surrounds me, there is nothing beyond her. The feeling of her body. All of my senses are centered around Elise.

Her hands slide up my arms before running down my back. Straightening, I pull my shirt over my head, wanting her hands on my skin. We're crossing every line today and I want to savor the moment. It may be the only one we have.

Elise sits up, her dress and bra following mine to the floor, leaving her only in her black lace panties. Groaning, I take in her peaked nipples. The perfect roundness of her breasts begs for my hands. She lays back down, her eyes hooded as she watches me, waiting. My eyes devour her as she's spread out beneath me, so close to completely bare but not close enough. I want to explore her entire body. My hands stroke the soft skin of her waist before moving to her breasts, massaging the perfect mounds. She arches up into me, those expressive green eyes never leaving my face.

Holding her gaze, I lean down to capture one hard bud, sucking and licking until she's writhing beneath me. I move to the other one before kissing my way down her body to the barely there fabric covering her sweet heat.

The idea of waiting to see her, taste her, any longer is unbearable, my hands pulling the fabric down her legs and tossing it to join the rest of the clothes on the floor.

Groaning, I stroke a finger over her, my cock throbbing at how wet she is. "Fuck, you're perfect." My words are guttural. We haven't spoken since we got in the car, but I can't keep silent anymore. Moving back up her body so I can look directly into her eyes, I practically growl, "Are you sure?"

Instead of responding, she reaches down, grabbing my erection through my boxer briefs and stroking. Her grasp is firm, sure, and if I lacked self-control, I'd be coming in my pants.

Grabbing her hand, I kiss her palm when she starts to protest. I stroke my finger through her wetness, moving it to circle her clit. The sound of her moans is erotic and everything. Pushing her thighs apart, I settle between them and stroke my tongue over her.

She tastes better than I ever imagined, and I lose myself in her, like a man who's starving.

"Young Jae..." She moans my name, the sound almost more than I can bear. Hearing my name from her lips in this moment, as she explodes around me, there will never be another person for me. I was delusional to think I could ignore my feelings forever. She's the only one I've ever truly seen.

I rip my boxers down my legs, positioning myself between her thighs. Grabbing myself, I stroke the head through her wetness, barely able to restrain myself from thrusting in when she lifts her hips into me.

Pulling away, I lean to the bedside table when her voice, thick with arousal, stops me.

"I have an IUD. And I'm clean. I've never..." She pauses. "I want to feel you. I need to."

Fuck.

All my restraint evaporates, I thrust into her in one quick motion, unable to take it slow. Her pussy clenches around me and I move. My lips find hers, our tongues moving as we flow together seamlessly. It's never been like this, passionate but somehow more. The feeling of being inside her is incredible. I'd be lying to myself if I said I hadn't fantasized about this, but it's better than I ever thought. The only thing that overshadows it is what it's doing to me to be with her like this after longing for more our entire friendship.

Her body quivers, my movements becoming jerkier as we both climb to the edge and fall over, her moans and whispers of my name piercing me as I come.

Collapsing onto my forearms, I brush a strand of sweat soaked hair from her forehead. Smiling, I brush my nose against hers. The nerves I thought I would feel at crossing this line are nowhere to be found, her expressive eyes telling me this meant as much to her as it did to me.

"Perfection," I whisper, kissing her softly before pulling out. Rolling to lay beside her, I start to protest when she gets out of bed. "Where do you—"

Elise laughs. "I will be back."

She heads into the bathroom, coming out less than three minutes later and climbing back into bed. I pull her into my arms, relishing the feeling of her there.

Elise smiles at me. "I guess the town's efforts in matchmaking finally paid off."

My lips quirk and I tap her nose. "It was inevitable. Between our friends, the town, and those tiny little shorts you love to wear, I never stood a chance."

She scrunches her nose. "You're one to talk with your tight T-shirts and those gray sweatpants."

Elise snuggles in closer, her laughter teasing my chest, and I feel myself hardening again. She stills, her eyes widening.

Propping her leg over my hip, I push into her again. I've been denying myself this for fifteen years, hell if I'm not going to be with her as much as I can. I just hope this isn't a whim, a momentary lapse that leads to my heart being broken later.

Chapter Eleven

Elise

I hear the bell ring from the kitchen in Perk Up. Mary calls back to let me know Adeline and Rae are here. It's been far too long since we've had a girls' night and since I have more free time, it was overdue.

Finishing up the last of the prep so everything is ready to go in the morning, I glance around the kitchen to ensure it's clean. Washing up, I hang my apron with one final check.

Having my afternoons free has been incredible and it feels like Mary has been here for years instead of mere weeks. Her cooking skills are phenomenal, and we have a great rotation of hot items, which more than pays for the cost of hiring her.

Leaving the kitchen, I smile at the gals. "Mary, everything is prepped for this evening and for in the morning, so there shouldn't be much to do after close. Call me if there's anything you need."

She smiles maternally. "I will be okay. You have fun."

With a wave, I follow my friends out the door.

"Brynne said she can't come for pedicures, but I think I managed to convince her to join us for dinner." Adeline's voice is disappointed, but I'm not surprised.

We opt to walk to the salon, enjoying the sunny day.

"I'm not surprised. She doesn't really like to be around crowds," I voice my thoughts. Sighing, I think about how isolated she is and frown. "I'm hoping maybe we can get her out of her shell a bit. Her family name follows her like a curse in her mind, but no one blames her for her father and brothers' issues with the law and overall horrendousness."

Rae hums in agreement, her fingers flying over her phone. "Sorry, I'm sending off a contract for a new graphic design client. I know I'm still in school, but things are really taking off. I didn't think people would want to hire someone who is still learning, but I was wrong."

"You've always been creative and it's not like you're starting from scratch." My words are strong. Rae comes across as confident, but sometimes she doubts herself. The work she's been doing speaks for itself, but on occasion she slips and needs a reminder.

We reach the salon, Tamarya greeting us as we head inside. She recently added a few pedicure chairs to the back area trying to increase tourist traffic in her salon.

"Ah! My guinea pigs. The girls are waiting in the back for you." She beams, her excitement palpable.

It doesn't take long for us to be seated with our feet soaking in hot water, the massagers in the chairs buzzing.

"How are things going with Young Jae?" Rae cocks her head, eyeing me.

It's been a couple weeks since things took a carnal turn, but I haven't told my friends yet. I don't know what Young Jae's thoughts are regarding our friendship and what the sex means, so I didn't text them. But I need their insight—just not right now.

Shrugging, I say easily, "Good. We've found our routine and I don't think I wake him up when I get ready for work anymore."

It's moments like these that I'm grateful I'm not a big blusher otherwise my lie would be revealed. I want to tell them, but not in front of three of the town's biggest gossips.

I see Rae eye Katie, Serena, and Beth. They're clearly listening intently as they work on our feet and she nods slightly.

We move on to talk about how things are with Adeline and Owen. Owen's mom moved into the apartment above Adeline's barn this spring.

"How is it having the potential future mother-in-law so close?" I ask.

It's hard for me to imagine having family nearby. My mom passed away when I was a child and my dad remarried and moved away as soon as I turned eighteen. He reaches out on my birthday and holidays, but our relationship has been strained due to his wife.

Adeline smiles fondly. "It's been good. She's very respectful, calling before she comes over and she never overstays her welcome."

"That's great. It's hard enough in a small town to have boundaries sometimes. Being within walking distance could be a disaster." Rae laughs, her family is tight-knit and she wouldn't have it any other way. But her dad rarely leaves the farm, and her mom is so busy with committees and town functions that she doesn't have time to push herself into her children's lives.

They talk back and forth about their families and it's hard not to feel that tug of missing out. I used to be close to my dad, but it's been so long that I forget what it's like.

Rae pauses, glancing at me. "Have you heard from your dad recently?"

Shaking my head, I shrug. "I heard from him at Christmas. Honestly, at this point I don't know why he bothers. You're all my family more than he is."

They nod, their expressions fierce. "He's missing out," Adeline says.

Smiling at my friends, I reset the massager in the chair as we talk and change the subject. He is missing out, and I'm so grateful to have such an incredible group of friends who are always there for me. We finish up, our toes gleaming with fresh polish.

Despite Tamarya's insistence that we were her test subjects, we paid her for the pedicures before returning to my place.

When I arrive home, I notice Young Jae has already left for dinner with his family. They all know I'm living with him, but don't know about the shift in our relationship. He's always been private about the women he sees, so it's not unusual, but part of me wonders if I am different or if we're just passing time.

The biggest question is, if he's just passing time, can we return to what we were before? I don't think my heart could take that.

The gals park on the driveway and follow me into the house through the garage. Kimchi comes racing down the stairs, excited to see me. She bounces around between us, not settling until we've all said hello.

"I will always be more of a cat person, but this dog makes me think I could do a dog too." Raelyn chuckles as we follow Kimchi to the kitchen.

Adeline grins. "I'm trying to convince Owen that goats are a good idea. He's not sold yet, but I always say it's better to ask for forgiveness than for permission."

Her eyes twinkle and I know she's already started looking at goats.

We come into the kitchen, ready to scrounge up some food when we stop. On the counter is a huge bouquet of dahlias and a huge spread of food. All covered and ready to go with a note that a fresh bottle of white wine is chilling in the fridge.

"Okay, this is amazing. Why aren't you with him again? He clearly cares about you as more than a friend." Rae unfreezes, moving forward to take the covers off the food.

It's everything needed to put together bibimbap.

"This smells incredible. What is it?" Adeline asks, looking at all the things laid out.

Instead of answering Rae, I show Adeline how to mix everything together.

The rice, veggies, bulgogi, egg, gochujang, and sesame oil all mix into the most delicious meal.

"This is one of my favorites. You can make it as spicy as you want." I finish putting everything together and they quickly make their own.

We're about to sit at the table with our food and full glasses of wine when the doorbell rings.

I set my dinner down and head to answer the door. Adeline and Rae speak in hushed tones, but I know it's about me and Young Jae.

Opening the door, I'm thrilled to see Brynne on the other side.

"Hey! We're so glad you came." Ushering her into the house, I show her how to make bibimbap before pouring her a glass of wine.

Despite the distraction, I feel Rae's eyes on me after she greets Brynne.

"So, why aren't you and Young Jae together? And don't give me the friend crap, this is more than 'just friends' behavior," Rae presses, not letting me avoid her question.

Chewing on my lower lip, I lift my gaze and smile. "We're sleeping together, have been for about two and a half weeks or so."

Their shrieks are loud as they start talking over each other and my smile won't go away. When they finally calm down, I fill them in on our dinner and the shift.

"I didn't say anything because we haven't talked about what we are. Are we friends with benefits until I move away? Are we dating? If we are, we haven't gone on any dates. Nothing has changed except now I've seen him naked." My smile falls a bit. "I want it to be more. I want something permanent. But it scares me that he doesn't feel the same."

They look at me empathetically. Understanding how hard it is to open yourself up to love and shifting relationships, even if it's in different ways.

"You never know until you have the conversation," Adeline points out, her voice soft.

Rae gestures to the table. "This doesn't say casual to me."

"Young Jae feels as deeply for you as you do for him. He has ever since we were in school." Brynne's raspy voice is quiet, but I know she means what she says.

Her words sink in. He's liked me since school? I don't think that's right, but I know he likes me now and that's enough.

I can see their point, but I'm not ready to ask the questions I know I will need to. "I'm just going to enjoy the moment for now and ask the questions later."

They exchange looks and I know they're worried about my heart, but my heart was Young Jae's a long time ago. It may have been dormant for a while, but it was always there, lingering beneath the surface.

Chapter Twelve

Elise

Young Jae's hand runs through the ends of my hair, the movement lulling me further into sleep. My body aches deliciously after several orgasms. I'm so blissed out, I don't think my legs would work to toss my PJs on.

His other hand starts tracing lazy patterns over my hip. Sighing, I snuggle into him even more and close my eyes. This doesn't feel temporary, but we still haven't talked about what we are. We've been doing this for a month now and life has been good. Our friendship is much like it's always been. We still have our Sundays on the lake or doing something active. We eat dinner every night and spend almost every evening together. But when we're out, it's the same as it was before we started sleeping together.

At home though, the touches are lingering. The kisses are frequent. And our sex life is incomparable. I've never felt like I've had the best of both worlds, but not knowing where his head is at is driving me crazy.

If I'm being honest, it bugs me a bit that we haven't gone on a true date, something outside of our routine.

"That's a big sigh." Young Jae's voice is low, his post-sex rumble the hottest sound I've ever heard. "What's wrong?"

I should tell him what I'm thinking, but the words won't come out. "Just can't seem to get out of my head. Maybe I need to do something fun tomorrow, help me clear my mind."

He's quiet.

Sighing, I kiss his neck before rolling out of bed to clean up. Taking my time with my nightly routine, it's about twenty minutes before I'm crawling back into bed.

"I took tomorrow off and booked something fun for us to do. Something you're going to love." He smiles, that dimple popping as I cozy up under the covers.

"It's a date," I murmur. It's the closest I get to telling him where I'm at, but it's something for now.

***

Young Jae pulls into a farm, no sign or anything.

Side-eyeing him, I don't say anything as we drive down a long gravel road. As I'm about to joke about whether he's lost, we pull into a clearing with a beautiful red barn and two horses saddled and tied at a hitching post.

Inhaling sharply, I stare. "We're going riding? You don't like horses."

He chuckles. "I like them when I'm on the ground, but I know you like riding and figured an hour in the saddle is worth seeing the look on your face right now."

It doesn't take long to run through the rules with the stable staff and get into the saddle, the black horse, Ebony, beneath me relaxes as we start moving. Patting her gently, I take the lead since I know Young Jae isn't confident in the saddle.

"I don't think I've been on horseback in probably six years. Thank you. I really needed this." Settling in, I follow the arrows guiding us over the vast property.

The buckskin Young Jae is on follows lazily and he soon relaxes into the ride. "I asked when I booked, and they offer lessons and will lease horses. If you're interested, I can forward you their different programs and costs."

Brushing my hair over my shoulder, I glance back at him and smile. "You're the best."

"I just want to see you happy."

His words go straight into my heart, giving me the warm fuzzies. I know how much he cares about me and this feels an awful lot like a date. Maybe I just need to stop questioning things and go with the flow.

We plod along in silence for a bit, my body moving easily with my horse.

"You know, this isn't so bad. The view's almost as nice as when you fall off your paddleboard and your T-shirt glues to your skin—almost." His tone is teasing, but when I look at him, his gaze is heated. "I find your confidence so sexy."

My body pulses in response, heat spreading as I feel his gaze continue to rake over me.

Laughing, I kick Ebony into a trot. "Stop that. We're going to enjoy this ride and then you're going to take me for dinner."

Young Jae clicks at his horse. After some awkward grunting and quicker steps follow behind me. Pressing my lips together to hold in my laugh, I stop my horse and wait for him to catch up.

"Dinner sounds good, but if you like having sex with me, please don't make me go that fast again." He grimaces, adjusting in the saddle.

I can't hold my laughter in anymore, leaning forward in the saddle, I clutch my stomach. "Oh my gosh. Okay, I promise."

We take it slow through the trails, talking about work and life. When we come out the end, disappointment fills me. A complete contrast from the relief on Young Jae's face.

"If you start riding again, I'm happy to watch you, but I think my butt is staying out of the saddle from now on." He dismounts with a grimace as soon as we're close to the hitching post where a staff member waits.

Grinning, I nod. "It's a deal."

Thanking the staff, I give the horses some pets before we get in the car to head out.

"There's a restaurant in Thistle Creek that I've heard is really good. It's called ThaiLicious. The family that owns it has been in town for a long time, and the restaurant is one of Alberta's top three Thai spots." Young Jae pulls out of the driveway. "Want to try it?"

"Absolutely."

The drive to Thistle Creek from the ranch is short and we talk the entire time. This feels like a date and a lot of the inner turmoil from before eases. Young Jae may not verbally express how he feels about me, but he shows it and maybe that's enough.

I have loved living with him and have felt more at home than I have in the past five years with Jake. When I think about moving out, it makes me sad.

I know I should be looking for places, but not much is popping up from my inquiries so I've basically hit pause. Only one possibility has arisen, and I'm supposed to go see it in a couple weeks. Part of me hopes it will fall through. Young Jae hasn't mentioned me leaving, so I don't feel as bad as I maybe should.

Chewing on my lower lip, I glance over at Young Jae. He's singing along to the radio, his hand tapping along on the steering wheel.

Despite our many years of friendship, maybe it's too soon to live together as more than friends anyway. We don't even know what we are yet and I'm overthinking everything. Except the sex, that has been great.

And the fact that our friendship seems steady as ever.

A laugh whooshes out of me. I'm being ridiculous.

"What's so funny?" Young Jae turns the already quiet music down even more.

Shaking my head, I mutter, "Nothing really. I was just thinking about how funny life is sometimes."

It's close enough to the truth that I don't feel like I'm lying to him, but not so truthful we have a conversation that could lead to answers I may not want.

He hums, reaching his hand over to rest on my leg. "Sometimes, I think things just work out how they're meant to."

Resting my hand over his, I squeeze it and agree.

ThaiLicious is packed, and when I say packed, I mean every table is full.

Gaping as Young Jae gives his name, stating he has a reservation, I smirk when he takes my hand and we follow the hostess back out onto the patio to an empty table overlooking the creek.

"Someone is full of surprises today." I'm beaming as he holds my chair out for me before sitting down.

He reaches across the table for my hand again, his thumb stroking over the sensitive skin. "I love seeing how happy and relaxed you are. You're more at ease than you've been in a long time and I never want that to disappear."

The server arrives to take our drink orders and I quickly scan the menu, ordering a Thai Iced Milk Tea. Young Jae orders the same and she leaves us to decide on dinner.

"It feels good that life is so amazing right now, but you know that along with the ups come the downs. And that's okay as long as my support network is there to help me through." Leaning back in my chair, I don't need to look at the menu. My favorite Thai dish is Panang Curry, and it's been ages since I've had any.

He looks pensive before nodding. "You're right. And you know we're always here for you."

The server returns with our drinks and we order. Young Jae gets my second favorite, red curry.

As she leaves once more, he shifts his chair to be next to mine, so we're looking over the creek. The patio is secluded with forested areas on either side and across from us. In the water, some ducks swim. Despite how packed it is, the noise of the people is a quiet hum. It's lovely.

"Today was just what I needed, thank you." Taking a cue from when he held my hand earlier, I lean into him and kiss his cheek. He drapes his arm over my shoulders pulling me in and I relax, laying my head on his shoulder. "I think you're right. I missed riding, so getting back into it would be good for me. I'm so used to being busy, having all this extra time doesn't feel right."

I feel his lips on the crown of my head.

"Did I just hear you say Young Jae was right?" We both stiffen at the familiar voice, I sit up as Ji Hoon pulls out the empty chair at our table and sits down. His eyes dance at us, taking in Young Jae's arm which hasn't moved.

I'm okay with people knowing about us but I'm still unsure about our future. Ignoring the anxiety in my belly, I nod. "You did. He took me to a stable for a trail ride today and has been telling me since I hired Mary at Perk Up I should do something for me with my free time."

Ji Hoon smiles at his brother, the affection and pride clear. "He is pretty smart, most of the time."

"What're you doing in Thistle Creek?" Young Jae asks after a few moments of pleasantries. No one talks about the elephant in the room, but I feel its weight.

Ji Hoon leans back, bracing his hands behind his head. "There's an auto supply shop here that can order the tools we need and we want to support locals, so I came to check it out. Liam should be here in a couple weeks and our focus will be on getting the shop put back together."

"It will be nice having a mechanic in town again," I agree, noticing he didn't say anything about why he was in ThaiLicious.

Our server arrives with our food, setting it in front of us.

"Well, I better be off. Enjoy your date." Ji Hoon stands, winking at our server before heading out.

Young Jae adjusts to start eating, but I don't. Chewing on my lip, I take a deep breath. "You know Ari will hear about this?" I murmur before digging into my food.

He shrugs. "Yeah, she would've heard about us eventually, right?"

"Sure, I guess. Eventually."

We dig in, sharing our dishes back and forth. I can see why it's rated so well.

"This is incredible. We definitely have to come back with our friends. They would love it." Young Jae scoops coconut rice and red curry, savoring each bite.

Mumbling in agreement, we easily polish off our food. The conversation shifts from horses to the redesign of the grain elevator and to things at home. It's easy and I love that adding sex to our relationship made it better while the other amazing parts stayed the same.

Chapter Thirteen

Young Jae

I'm the last one to arrive at Owen's, even Ji Hoon's car is outside. It's been almost two weeks since he ran into Elise and me on our date and I haven't been harassed or questioned about it, but I'd be an idiot to think I'm not walking into the lion's den right now.

Honestly, I'm glad he saw us. I don't want things with Elise to feel like a dirty secret, but I also know people in a small town talk. They may want us together, but the fact that she and Jake broke up mere months ago will be cause for speculation about my relationship with her and when it started. I could not care less about people talking about me, but I don't want Elise to have to deal with the small town gossip more than the whisperings we're used to.

I walk into the kitchen, catching the tail end of a conversation about the house Cameron and Rae are moving into and all their plans around the property. The energy shifts as soon as they see me, and I have three smirking faces staring at me.

"You finally took the leap, we hear." Cam is the first to say anything while Ji Hoon grins at me before grabbing another beer.

"About damn time," Owen adds.

Rolling my eyes, I take the bottle Ji Hoon hands me, pop the top, and take a sip. "If you recall, Elise has been in a relationship for five years. It's not like I was going to put her in a position that would make her uncomfortable and jeopardize our friendship."

Switching to Korean, I call Ji Hoon a gossip and tell him that when it's his turn, he better watch out.

He laughs. "Yeah, that's never gonna happen."

"When did it start?" Owen cuts in.

Taking another drink, I think back to the night Rae and Adeline booked us the table at Cliff's. "About a month and a half ago. Ever since your significant others decided to book us one of the booths Cliff's has."

They laugh, clinking their glasses together. "Wait until they find out. They're going to be thrilled."

I feel my lips pull into a smug smile. "They just had a girls' night not too long ago, I'm pretty sure they already know."

Laughing as they pull out their phones and start texting, I make my way to the table where everything is laid out for poker.

"So, what are you then? Because Adeline mentioned that Elise is going to look at an apartment next week. Please tell me this is more than sex because I'd hate to see you and her ruin what you both have wanted for so long." Owen sits down, picking up the cards and shuffling.

Setting my beer down harder than I mean to, I stare. "She is? She never told me that."

Clenching my jaw, I try to ignore the way the beer has turned sour in my gut. I don't want her to move. I love having her at home with me and she belongs there. If she moved, the house would feel so empty.

"Well, have you told her where your head is? Or are you sleeping together and living life as you always have?" Cam interjects as he sits next to me.

Brows furrowing, I think about the past month and a half. He's right, aside from the one date night and sleeping together, everything else has basically remained the same. The physical aspect has been more than sex, so I assumed she knew I am serious about this, but I guess assuming shit is just idiotic.

"I'm a dumbass."

They all agree.

As Owen deals out the cards, the conversation shifts. But my head is still on Elise.

Is she looking at apartments because she thinks I'm not serious? Or because she's not taking what we have seriously?

***

I'm waiting for Elise with dinner on the table when she gets home from work. After guys' night last night, I didn't say anything. I needed to see if there was any indication that this was nothing but sex to Elise, but even after two a.m. sex and breakfast this morning, I can't tell.

She comes in the door, her voice carrying as she greets Kimchi. I love the sound of her coming home after work. She's always so happy to see us and it feels good knowing that now she comes in and kisses me before we have dinner.

Elise comes through the door, a soft smile on her lips as she sees me with dinner. Her kiss is short, but it's almost the one I look forward to most every day.

"It was so busy at Perk Up today. I'm really seeing all the work we've put into the new menu items. Mary has been such a blessing." She sighs as she sits, the sound pure happiness.

I don't want to bombard her as soon as she comes in the door. We start eating and I watch her, wondering what she's thinking.

"How was your day?" she asks as she finishes telling me about some of the new recipes they want to try.

"It was good, lots of meetings and then I worked on the design. Kimchi and I took a walk at lunch." It feels weird to talk about the normal, mundane things when this pit is sitting in my chest.

She's quiet as she eats and I can't take it anymore.

Setting my fork down, I lean back in my chair. "So, I heard you're looking at an apartment next week. Why didn't you tell me?"

I try to keep my tone neutral, but Elise knows me too well and sees right through it.

"I had it booked a while ago, before things shifted with us, and never canceled. I wasn't sure whether this was serious or not since we hadn't talked about it, so I figured I would go see it. I can always turn it down." She shifts in her seat, awkwardness filling the air for the first time between us.

"Are we just casual?" I ask. I don't want us to be, but that's moot if she doesn't want anything serious after ending a five-year relationship.

She lets out a heavy breath, her gaze intent on mine. "I don't want this to be casual. I've never been happier."

The tension flows out of my body so hard, I slump in my chair before jumping up. I close the distance between us, leaning down to kiss her with all the emotion I've been holding in. "Thank goodness. I want to give this a shot, a real shot because I'm happier than I've ever been."

"Me too." She sighs, beaming at me.

Her arms wrap around my neck as she kisses me back and I realize she was holding the same tension I was.

"We probably should've just talked about this earlier." Her laugh is breathless as I release her and go back to my chair.

Running a hand down my face, I grin and shake my head. "Yep. But I was worried about pressuring you."

"And I was worried about scaring you away." She laughs, picking at her food.

Leaning onto my elbows, I am serious as I say, "I want you to stay. I don't want you to move out."

The smile that curves is brilliant. "Sounds good."

"We basically skipped all the awkward get-to-know-you stuff anyway. Well, except physically, you have surprised me there a little." She covers her hands with her face, laughing.

Shushing me, she takes a bite of food and just shakes her head. "I have no regrets. Things are more than satisfying." She smirks, running her fingers over her collarbone. "And now that I'm not wondering where your head is at, it's only going to get better."

Heat rushes through me and if it wasn't for all the food on the table, I would be shoving it clear and taking her up on that.

"Is it weird that our relationship feels more long term than it technically is?" I love it, but I don't want her to feel like she's missing out on anything.

Elise taps her lips, but the corners are lifting, which gives her away. "No. But I want to make sure we stay adventurous and go on dates. We have stayed in our same routine except for adding sex, and I want intimacy outside of sex. I want to be a couple."

It's a relief that we're finally communicating about what we want instead of trying to prevent the other from feeling pressured.

"You're right. We definitely need to do that. I honestly didn't want you to have to deal with the town gossiping about how things with Jake ended and we started dating, seeing as they've been speculating about us for years." It made sense in my head, but I realize how idiotic it was when I say it out loud.

She rolls her eyes. "The town is going to talk regardless. They're going to be thrilled their matchmaking efforts worked out. So it is what it is."

We move on, planning our Sunday together. Life feels so good and I can't wait to show the world she's mine.

Chapter Fourteen

Elise

The morning sun shines into the room, but that's not what woke me up. Young Jae's lips press a soft kiss on my shoulder, his hand low on my stomach and his cock hard in my back.

Moaning, I roll over, gripping him in my palm as he kisses my jaw toward my lips. Releasing him, I cover my mouth and shake my head.

"I need to freshen up for this." Rolling away from him, I dodge his hand and race into the bathroom, laughing at his groan.

"I don't care about your morning breath," he calls through the door.

Yelling back I say, "Well, I do!"

His laughter carries through as I freshen up, but he turns serious when I come back into the bedroom completely naked. The trail of heat his eyes leave as they devour me hits me straight in the core and I know I'm slick and ready for him.

Crawling over the bed, I nudge him onto his back. I'm not in the mood for a ton of foreplay, my pussy aching for him. I've felt insatiable since we finally talked about what we're doing, every touch holding more meaning to me.

My heart belongs to this man, and even though I'm not ready to share that, I can tell him with my actions.

Straddling his hips, I grip him, positioning myself. Sinking down onto him, I moan as he fills me. Bracing my hands on either side of his head, I kiss him as I start to move. The angle creates delicious friction of him moving in me and the pressure on my clit.

Every time his hips thrust up to meet mine, every stroke of his hands over my thighs, my breasts, and when he links our hands together, it brings me closer to the edge.

My heart is full as we move together, my climax building. And when I look into his eyes, I think I see the same love radiating back at me.

This is the love I've always craved. The love I never truly knew. And it's everything.

***

Young Jae's lips devour mine as he lifts me onto the counter. His hands slide up my shirt.

Giggling, I press my hands into his chest, fisting his shirt. "They're going to arrive any moment," I mutter against his lips before opening to him. He tastes so good, like wine and chocolate.

He moves to my jawline, kissing the sensitive spot under my ear. "You started it."

The doorbell rings, interrupting us.

Young Jae presses his forehead to mine, groaning, before setting me back on the floor to straighten my shirt as he goes to greet our friends.

Their voices carry through, greeting Young Jae and then Kimchi as well. As I adjust myself and smooth my hair, I hear, "Yo, Jae... You have lipstick smudges around your mouth and down your neck." Owen's voice carries, sounding like he's barely repressing laughter.

"What, you don't like my new look?" Young Jae quips back and I hear him go into the main floor bathroom.

Our friends pile in for our triple date. It's the soft launch of our relationship and I know they're all excited based off the texts from Rae and Adeline.

Before they can say anything about my lipstick on Young Jae, I say, "Hey! Pizza is in the kitchen, and tons of drinks are in the fridge."

They all look at me knowingly, smirking.

"We hope we're not interrupting anything." Rae laughs, not letting me get away with my attempt to redirect their attention.

Resisting the urge to stick out my tongue like a child, I shake my head. "Not at all."

She laughs knowingly, heading into the kitchen to grab some food.

Young Jae comes into the room, face cleared of any lipstick, sending a wink my way before asking the guys if they want a beer. The three of them head into the kitchen, leaving Adeline and me in the dining room.

"The town is abuzz after seeing you walking and holding hands." She smiles knowingly. "From what I can tell, everyone is so happy. According to one of our teen volunteers, people have been 'shipping' the two of you forever."

Chuckling, I shrug not knowing what else to do. "I'm not surprised after the matchmaking attempts. It will die down eventually, as you know."

She groans, remembering when she was the topic of the town gossip. "You're right. Eventually they will move on. But seriously, we're all so happy for you. When it's right, it's right and finally the timing worked out."

We all settle in the living room, spread around with our food. I can practically hear the squealing going on in Rae and Adeline's heads when Young Jae runs his fingers down my arm as he passes me.

Soon the conversation shifts away from our relationship to other things, like Cam and Rae's upcoming move.

"We can't wait to host a housewarming party. It's my dream house," Rae gushes, going into her plans for an attic office.

I know how much she wishes some of those rooms would be for children, but her struggles to get pregnant are a huge part of why she and Cam split up so many years ago. I'm glad to see her brainstorming ideas like a cat room.

That's something Young Jae and I have never discussed, it's never really come up, but I'm not sure where he stands on kids. I'm so used to my life how it is, I think having kids would be a hard transition.

The evening flies by and soon our friends are leaving. As we shut the door, Young Jae turns to me. "Now, let's finish what we started."

He bends down, quickly flipping me onto his shoulder and lifting before I can make a peep. Instead of heading upstairs, he strides into the kitchen and plants me on the counter, lifting my shirt over my head.

My bra falls to the floor next and his lips are on my nipple before I've hardly had time to process. My head falls back as he explores my body, building me up to the point I feel like I may black out from need.

"Please," I moan.

Young Jae doesn't need to be asked twice. He lifts me down quickly working my pants off, turning me so my elbows are resting on the counter.

"Stay." His voice is guttural as he frees his cock and thrusts into me hard and deep. My body is electric as he moves, his hand sliding over my hip and down, the first brush of his fingers over my clit sending shock waves through me.

"So fucking wet," he groans, working me until the delicious explosion of my orgasm rips through me. I drop onto the counter, unable to hold myself as he moves. He comes, his body pressed over me, his forehead pressed into my back as his body quakes.

My legs are jelly as he pulls out, so he turns me, picks me up and carries me to the bathroom. "I'm pretty sure I'm broken," I mutter as he turns on the water.

"Oh?" His voice is full of humor.

"I can barely move and I already want you inside me again." Lifting my head, I eye him hungrily. I've never been so insatiable, but I can't get enough.

He laughs. "I think I can make that happen."

Chapter Fifteen

Elise

Young Jae brushes my hair behind my ear. "I love waking up next to you every day." His voice rumbles, still raspy from sleep.

Snuggling in, I kiss his chest. Taking a deep breath, I look up at him. "I love you."

He smiles, his hand cupping my cheek. "Saranghae."

The Korean for I love you caresses me. I can feel myself beaming at him.

"So, I was thinking, we need to move the rest of your stuff in here. You still go into the spare room to grab fresh clothes every day."

Laughing, I point at his closet. "That's because you have as many clothes as I do. Where am I supposed to put them?"

He props himself up onto his elbow. "You have forgotten I'm an architect. I was thinking we should do some minor renos, making the closet bigger. This room is unnecessarily huge, and we have the space."

I can't stop the smile that forms. "Let's plan it."

Young Jae twines his fingers with mine, falling serious. "I do have one thing I've been thinking. I heard Rae tell Adeline she thinks we would have cute kids.

I've never really seen a future with children. I just realized I don't know your thoughts on that."

Stroking my thumb over his hand, I can feel the apprehension in his body. This is a deal breaker for so many couples.

"I've always been neutral about having kids. I'm happy with how our life is and wouldn't feel like I'm missing out on anything by not having children. It's why I got the IUD."

"So you would be okay if we didn't have children? I don't want them. I love our life as it is, but we need to be on the same page." Young Jae's voice is firm. He needs an answer. A clear one.

"I am fine not having children. Besides, we have Kimchi. She's enough." I give him a gentle smile. I mean it. I don't need to have children. As long as we have each other.

He relaxes, moving on to some other ideas he has to make the house ours rather than his house that I've moved into. As we talk, I am so grateful for how thoughtful he always is. He hasn't changed how he is or who he is as we develop our relationship, still the same kind and considerate man I knew as a friend, but even more so.

Kimchi shoves herself between us, annoyed at the lack of attention she's getting. Laughing, I pet her and coo at her.

Young Jae's phone rings, unusual considering it's before working hours, so he peeks at it. "It's my mom."

He answers in Korean, I can't hear what she's saying, but my name comes through the speaker and she's talking faster than normal, which means she's mad or excited.

They talk back and forth for a while, and I hear enough of the conversation to pick up that his mom is disappointed he didn't tell her about us and she wants us to come for a family dinner on Saturday after I'm done work.

Young Jae looks at me, questioning. Nodding, I smile as he confirms and then hangs up.

"Well, my mom is happy I'm finally settling down and not wasting my time and 'good looks' being alone." He shakes his head.

Laughing, I roll onto my stomach and run my fingers over his chest. "I'm just glad she's happy."

"Are you kidding? She's your biggest fan. I had no doubt she would be happy." He reaches for me, but his alarm goes off. Groaning, he silences it. "Well, I guess that's a no for a morning quickie."

Jumping out of bed, I tease, "Since it's my day off, maybe I will just walk around the house naked. Taunt you all day."

He throws a pillow at me but grins. "Try it, see what happens."

We finish getting ready, eating a quick breakfast before he heads into a busy day. The grain elevator rebuild is in full swing and he is constantly assessing his plans to ensure nothing needs tweaking.

Despite it being my day off, I head to Perk Up for a coffee and to see how Mary's visit with Morgan went. She went to see her in Thistle Creek and from the sounds of it, her life there has been a bit of an adjustment.

Perk Up is quiet when I arrive, the before work crowd is already gone. Mary is cleaning the tables when I come in.

"Aren't you supposed to be relaxing?" she teases.

Pressing my hand into my chest, I look at her appalled. "What? I can't come into my shop on my day off?"

Mary smirks at my fake offense. "As long as you're still relaxing."

"I came for coffee and treats. And to see how your visit to Thistle Creek went." Going behind the counter, I prep what I want as she talks.

"I don't know. She seems a little overwhelmed with school. I take it not everyone has welcomed her with open arms. And the place she's staying, the farmer whose land it is, he's a bit intense. Nice, but intense." Mary's brows pinch together. "I wonder if something is going on with them, but Morgan said no."

Leaning against the counter, I frown. "That's too bad the welcome isn't warm. Hopefully they come around soon. It's an adjustment, I know small towns do things a little differently. But Morgan has a good head on her shoulders, she will figure it out."

Mary agrees half-heartedly and I bet it's hard to turn off the motherly worry.

Before we can talk about it more, the bell jingles and Ari comes in.

"Elise, thank goodness. I need your insight." She looks flustered. "Mary, I need the biggest caramel macchiato that you can make me. And anything sweet to go with it. Please."

Mary busies herself making Ari's drink as we head to a table.

"I'm so glad Young Jae finally got his head out of his butt and took your relationship to the next level." She smiles at me, her expression happy but I still see the strain around her eyes. "Two older brothers and I finally get a sister."

Mary comes to the table with her order.

"Mary, you're a goddess. Thank you." Ari sips at her macchiato and sighs heavily.

"I'm happy to be your sister." Watching her face, I see the downward pull of her lips even though she tries to hide it. "What's going on?"

It's unusual for Ari to be anything but smiling, so her expression worries me.

She sighs, resting her chin in her palm. "My parents refuse to retire, and whenever I try to make suggestions about how we can improve the inn, they shrug it off like I'm still twenty instead of twenty-seven with a business degree. Young Jae tried to talk to Eomma, but she got mad at him. Ji Hoon was able to make a little headway, but they still won't commit. I know it's unfair to ask, but I was hoping you could mention retirement at dinner. In that subtle way I suck at."

Grimacing, I set my coffee down. "I don't know, Ari. It's not really my place."

"But that's the thing, you don't have to say anything directly about retiring. It could be something about experiences or trips. But they will know what I'm getting at if I try to bring anything like that up." She slumps in the seat. "I'm ready to run the inn on my own. They don't bug Young Jae about his stuff. And they're staying out of Ji Hoon's way, even though his mysterious business partner has yet to arrive. But despite all the things I've managed to implement, they won't let go, not even to semi-retire."

Her voice pitches higher as she talks, the stress and frustration clear.

"Let me see what I can do, but I'm not promising anything." I sigh. What a way to jump into things with the Chois as Young Jae's girlfriend, not just friend.

"You're the best almost sister-in-law ever." Ari beams at me, the strain dissipating as though I've magically pulled off what she wants.

"Don't get your hopes up. All of you are stubborn and you inherit that from your parents," I warn.

She laughs, waving me off. "No one can say no to you, especially not my mother."

***

Saturday is busy at Perk Up, but my mind is occupied with dinner. I still haven't figured out what to say to the Chois to help Ari out and I don't want to involve Young Jae because he will jump down her throat. Nerves must be getting to me, because I've been feeling queasy all day.

After I close up, I race home to change and we arrive at the Choi's for dinner.

"Why do you seem so nervous? You've been to our family dinners before." He reaches for my hand, squeezing gently.

"It's not the same as your girlfriend. I'm excited, but it's different." It's partially the truth.

He pulls me into his arms, kissing me softly. "It will be great. You're already family."

We head inside, delicious smells greeting us as we come in the door, followed by his mom rushing to me.

"Elise! It's been too long." She switches between English and Korean as she ushers me into the house and to the dining room. Mr. Choi, Ji Hoon, and Ari are already seated at the table, but there's still one empty spot. "We're just waiting for Liam and then we can eat. Eat lots, I haven't been able to cook for you in a long time."

She eyes Young Jae who laughs and holds up his hands. "She's busy, Eomma."

"He's right. I finally hired someone so I can reduce my hours. It's going so well, I might consider hiring someone else in a year to take over the morning shifts and reduce my hours to baking and management." I fill them in on what we've been doing at the coffee shop and my goal to semi-retire in five years.

Mrs. Choi listens, her expression proud. She's watched me grow up and was always like the mom I didn't have. I'm glad to still have that.

"That's good. More time for you and Young Jae." She approves.

My heart thrumming a little faster, I casually ask, "Have you and Mr. Choi thought about what you want to do when it's time to retire? I saw a really neat tour company catering specifically to retired couples. They have a lot of options."

Mr. Choi lights up, but doesn't say anything as he glances at his wife. She looks over at Ari, who is busy on her phone, but I know she is attuned to the conversation.

"We have talked about it but haven't decided when the time is right. We don't want to abandon Ari with the inn, leaving her on her own." Mrs. Choi watches as Ari stands up, typing on her phone.

Resting my hand on Young Jae's leg, I tap my fingers as I try to think of the best way to encourage her without overstepping.

"I get that. My friend Adeline raves about the service she got when she stayed at the inn, she had nothing but good things to say about Ari and her experience." Trying another approach, I feel like I'm failing.

Young Jae rests his hand on mine, linking our fingers. "I think Ari has it under control. She has great ideas. Besides, you and Appa retiring doesn't mean she can't ask for help if she ever needs it. We've all pitched in before."

"I think we should retire. I'm tired and I want to spend time with my wife, not working," Mr. Choi pipes up, crossing his arms as he meets Mrs. Choi's gaze.

She frowns a moment, watching as Ari comes back in the room. "Perhaps you're right. We can discuss this later, yeobo."

The affectionate word softens the sharpness of her tone. Her wanting to stay on comes from a place of love, but also fear. They've been working so much of their lives, I can see how hard it is to let go.

Ari's lips twitch as she tries to hold back her joy. And Mr. Choi nods, satisfied.

Before we can say anything else, the doorbell rings.

"That'll be Liam." Ji Hoon gets up and goes to let his friend in. "Impeccable timing, dude."

"Sarcasm?" An Irish accented voice carries down the hall.

Ari freezes, paling a little as she turns her gaze to Ji Hoon and the tall, redheaded man following him into the room.

"This is Liam." Ji Hoon introduces us all in turn.

No one else catches it, but I see him double take when Ji Hoon introduces Ari, his eyes going back to her as he takes a seat.

That's interesting. Ari stares down at the table as we start eating, picking at her food until everyone is done.

"I don't feel well, please excuse me." She doesn't wait for an acknowledgment before bolting out of the room.

Everyone gapes after her.

"I ran into her earlier today and she said she's had a headache all day. I'm guessing it never went away." I cover for her. Liam glances at her empty chair, his lips pressed into a firm line.

Ji Hoon shrugs it off, talking with Liam and his parents.

My stomach turns a bit, the nausea I've been fighting all day returning with a vengeance.

"You okay?" Young Jae notices my discomfort.

"Yeah, I thought I wasn't feeling well because I was nervous, but I wonder if I'm fighting a bug." Rubbing my stomach, I frown.

Young Jae excuses us and we head home. As he lets Kimchi out, I race to the bathroom, barely making it as I start retching.

If I'm thinking about it, my stomach has been more sensitive all week, which is really unusual. I rarely feel nauseous. I don't even remember the last time I had a stomach flu.

Sitting back, I grab some tissues to wipe my face. Even on my period I rarely have PMS. My heart almost stops as I roughly calculate. Am I supposed to be on my period?

Panic fills me and I rush to the guest ensuite, digging into the back of the cupboard. I dig out the pregnancy test I had left over from a while back when I had a scare and quickly brush up on the instructions.

"Everything okay?" Young Jae knocks, concern filling his voice.

I finish peeing as I respond I'm fine.

Flipping it face down, I wash up as I wait for the timer to go off.

When it does, I cross my fingers it's negative. Turning it over, I slump in relief. The single line is clear as day. Usually my periods are fairly light, but on occasion, I don't really have one because of my IUD. This must just be one of those times.

"Thank goodness," I mutter, burying the test in the trash. The last thing I need is to deal with an unwanted pregnancy.

Chapter Sixteen

Young Jae

Elise shivers despite the heavy blanket over her. A damp sheen covers her body. Tucking the blanket around her, I quietly shut the door to let Kimchi out and make some tea.

I quickly let my boss know I'm taking a sick day and set about making some soup and other foods to help Elise feel better.

As I cook, I call Mary.

"Hello?" Her voice answers, surprisingly alert for the early hour.

"Hi, Mary. It's Young Jae. Elise is really sick and won't be able to make it today. I'm not sure if you're able to—"

I hear her start moving. "I will take care of Perk Up. Tell her to rest and not to worry."

"Thanks, Mary." Hanging up, I finish prepping the bone broth and add it to the rice that's done in the cooker.

Kimchi waits patiently to be fed as I strain the broth.

Grabbing her bowl, I smile as she dances while I scoop her food, sitting patiently as I set it down. Scratching her head, I cue her to start eating.

Washing up, I grab some meds, pour the broth over rice and head back upstairs.

Elise is sitting up, her face pale.

"I called Mary, she's looking after the shop. And I took the day off so I can get you anything you need whenever you need it." Sitting next to her, I hand her the meds and the tea I made.

She leans back into the pillows with a sigh. "Thank you."

Taking the tea, I set it down and start feeding her the rice and soup. "This is bone broth. It's nice and mild. I always got this when I was sick as a child."

Elise hums as she eats. "It's perfect. Thank you."

After she finishes eating, I fluff her pillows, and she lies down, falling asleep almost right away. Brushing the hair from her face, I lean down to kiss her cheek.

Clearing the dishes, I get the kitchen cleaned up before grabbing my laptop and heading back to bed. Kimchi is curled up next to her. I settle in, working on the renovation plans for the bedroom, ready for when she needs me again.

***

The next few days are spent looking after Elise and cleaning around the house. I move my stuff into the guest room she was occupying when she first moved here, Owen agreeing to fit us into his schedule for the closet remodel.

With the grain elevator in full swing, my day-to-day is a lot lighter, so I check into work when necessary but haven't taken on any new projects.

By the end of the week Elise is feeling better and back at work.

That evening, I make a special dinner. All week she lived off the bone broth and rice, her stomach unable to handle more. Now that she's feeling better, I want to spoil her.

I start with seared scallops in a citrus sauce, with a mushroom risotto, and a fresh salad topped with walnuts and a light dressing. Instead of buying premade dressings, I make everything from scratch.

Setting the table, I add the bouquet of dahlias I bought and a couple long-stemmed candles.

By the time I hear her come in the door, her voice greeting Kimchi, the table is set and everything is ready.

Elise comes in, her eyes widening at the dinner before her. "Wow. What's the occasion?"

Opening my arms, I hug her close and kiss her, before holding her chair out for her. "I wanted to make a special dinner now that you're feeling better. I know your diet this week has been minimal, so I wanted to treat you. Besides, we haven't really been able to spend quality time since you really needed your rest, and I missed you."

I point to all the dishes and tell her what each one contains.

"This is incredible. I love you. Thank you for taking care of me this week, I feel like I should be the one cooking you a fancy dinner. I didn't even bring dessert." She pouts adorably, loading her plate with each of the dishes.

Beaming, I say, "I made apple crumble."

Her mouth drops. We both enjoy cooking, but it's no secret that desserts are out of my comfort zone, as is baking. "I can't wait."

We dive in, her eyes closing as she takes the first bite of scallop.

"This is incredible. Are you sure you don't want to do a pop up at Perk Up? I'm pretty sure you could be a chef and get a Michelin Star if you weren't an architect." She eats eagerly, appreciating every bite.

Watching her eat the food that I cooked, I can't imagine sharing this with anyone else. "I prefer to cook for the people I love. That's enough for me."

"Mary did an incredible job while I was recovering. She's the best person I could've found to help me." Elise fills me in on how things went, Mary opting to work the full days instead of reducing hours. "We're doing so well, I'm going to draft up a wage increase. She's definitely earned it. My profits are up twenty-three percent and we're busier than ever. Usually, it's tourists who are staying in town and the townsfolk who come in, but now we even have guests coming in just to try my desserts or the menu items."

Pride fills me. "That's amazing. I am happy everything worked out so well."

"It made me think about your friend in Mistik Ridge. I was wondering if there was a way I could help her without overstepping. The property is beautiful, but I think it's too much for one person." She starts thinking out loud about seeing if Tash would want some of her baked goods to offer specials on certain days of the week.

Her heart is so kind, the fact that she wants to find out how to share her success to help someone she met once, is one of the reasons I love her. "I will forward you her contact info. It's worth offering."

We finish dinner, and despite my insistence that she go relax, she refuses and does dinner clean up. Thankfully I had the foresight to do most of it beforehand.

"Would it be okay to wait for dessert? Maybe we can take Kimchi for a walk. I feel a little trapped after being in the house for almost a week." She stretches after turning on the dishwasher, her neck cracking.

Kimchi dances at the word walk, so we clip her to her leash and head out.

Holding Elise's hand, we greet our neighbors as we pass. Our relationship is still a hot item of discussion, but thankfully aside from some grins and knowing looks, everyone waits until we pass to talk.

Elise laughs. "I love small towns. I feel like we have our own cheer team."

Chuckling at the description, I sigh. "That's true, but it would be nice if something else stole their attention. I want to revel in our relationship, not be under a microscope for every move. I went into the jewelry store the other day for a watch battery and when I left there was an awkward crowd of people trying to look busy."

"I can only imagine."

We finish our walk and eat dessert on the couch, watching another reality show Elise suckered me into. Before the episode finishes, she falls asleep on the couch. I lower the volume, cleaning up the dishes and resetting the house while the show plays before lifting her and carrying her to bed.

She probably overdid it at work, since she gave Mary the day off to make up for all her time away. As I tuck her in, she doesn't even stir as I close the blinds and call Kimchi to the bed.

Hopefully she feels better for Sunday. I have a fun date planned.

Chapter Seventeen

Elise

Over the next week, I get my strength back. Young Jae is attentive, wanting to pamper me. His care while I was sick was more than I expected and every time we experience something we haven't in our relationship, it heals a part of me I didn't realize needed healing.

The more I've thought about offering to partner with Tash, the more I'm excited about it. But I don't want to just text her without a plan, so I sit down with my laptop to create a presentation.

As I work, I also think about offering to collaborate with Ari. She reached out while I was sick to tell me that her parents have finally decided to set up a transition plan for retirement. It feels good knowing that their parents are going to finally live their life outside of work and Ari will have the creative freedom to make decisions for the business she is inheriting.

She seemed a little off when we chatted, but was adamant that she's fine, just occupied with the transition.

Mary comes over to the table as I work, bringing me coffee. "How's it going?"

"Good. I think I'm almost done." I angle my laptop to show her the document I'm making with seasonal specialties I can cater to the inn while promoting the shop. "I don't want them to have the same product, so I'm trying to set up a customizable plan that we would collaborate on."

She reads over my shoulder as I wait anxiously.

"It's brilliant. And what a way to showcase other small businesses. If there's anything I can do to help, please let me know." Mary smiles, and I know she's not just saying that. One thing I've discovered about her is that she is always honest, even when you don't want to hear what she has to say.

The bell rings, a group of girls comes in and she heads to the counter.

I pull up my email, drafting a letter to Tash and attaching the proposal. I do the same for Ari. Leaning back with a sigh, I close my laptop and hope they consider my offer. If I've learned anything from hiring Mary and expanding the menu, taking chances like these makes work more fulfilling.

***

Tash stands on the porch of her inn, waving as I get out of my car. "Elise, it's good to see you."

I grab the folder of ideas I've been brainstorming and join her. "You too. I'm so glad you agreed to meet with me."

"The proposal you sent was intriguing, and I don't see the harm in going over things. Let's head inside, I have an office at the back of the house. We can go over things, finalize the plan, and then I will give you a tour." I follow her into the inn. As we head to the back of the house, I see a fat orange cat lounging on a piano bench.

He hisses and swats at me.

"That's grumpy George. Despite his awful manners, guests actually really love him and get a kick out of his angry demeanor." She pets him, the rumbling purrs at odds with his earlier hiss. "I'm the only one he likes. I rescued him from a coyote when he was maybe two years old and abandoned on the property. We somehow end up with a lot of abandoned animals here. A few years back someone dropped off a horse in the old horse pen."

Gaping at her, I ask, "What did you do?"

"Well, at the time, same as now, I couldn't afford the expense of such a large animal. I can barely keep afloat as it is. I called a local ranch and they came and got her. They're regular guests at the inn. The Hyatt family, they're what help keep me afloat." She gestures around her. I can see the work she's put into maintaining the place, but there's also wear.

"What happened? Young Jae said he met you shortly after you bought it and it was doing well." I soften my voice, not wanting to seem judgemental, but it doesn't make sense. Tash obviously cares for the place.

She sighs, her lips pulling down. "The building is old, and it was never maintained properly. Which I wasn't aware of when I bought it. It wasn't until a pipe burst that the plumber told me I had to redo a lot of structural stuff. Plumbing, electrical, there was some rotting that was never dealt with. I had to shut down large chunks of space at a time, which reduced capacity. And I was never able to financially recover. Then you add in the normal wear and tear, which is a huge deal when you've gone hundreds of thousands of dollars into debt."

Her eyes are glassy as she looks at me. "I've been pestered to sell it by a guy I know. His family used to own it. I worry I may not be able to resist for long."

Tsking empathetically, I follow her into her office and sit in one of the chairs. "What about taking on a partner? Someone who has the cash flow but doesn't want to be involved in the day-to-day."

She grabs a tissue, wiping her eyes, the weight heavy on her shoulders. So different from the woman reflected in the photos around her. "I have been looking around. So far, I only have one solid possibility, but they want to stay anonymous until I sign off on it. That worries me, but I may not have a choice."

It hurts my heart to think that she's struggling so much. "Well, let's see if we can figure out a way to get some business building up. Let's go through my proposal together and we can tweak as necessary."

We dive in, developing strategies to promote having Perk Up goodies at the Mistik Ridge Inn, including some mock-ups Rae did of the promotional material I would post in the shop.

Tash gets more and more excited as we go through. "This is great. If you can draft a contract and send it over, we can make it official."

I grin at her. "I will! Now, I'd love to get a tour."

She shows me around, her pride shining through as she shows me the rooms she has been able to upgrade and talks about her vision if things improve. I make a mental note to book a stay for me and Young Jae, wanting to support her how we can.

The drive home has me in my head about ways that I can try and help her or even other small businesses. I know how hard it is to build and maintain a business on your own. And just how hard it is to ask for help when needed.

Before heading home, I swing by the inn to give Ari her version of the paperwork I had drafted. She said she's also interested, but wants to look through it on her own and we can discuss once her parents are officially retired, so I need to follow up.

"Elise, my hero!" She bounces around the counter, jumping to give me a hug. "If Young Jae doesn't marry you, I just might."

Laughing, I hug her back. "Even if he doesn't, I can't foresee a future without Young Jae. Maybe hold out for your right person."

She cringes. "Most of the men in town I know too well. And the ones I don't aren't an option." Her face clouds a bit.

"Liam?"

She balks at me. "Who said Liam? Besides, he's like ten years older than me and Ji Hoon's best friend. I'm pretty sure Ji Hoon would end up in jail and Liam six feet under."

Smirking at her, I say coyly, "Yeah, maybe. But I'm more observant than your brothers. We will see what happens."

Mrs. Choi comes in, so I change the subject.

"Elise, thank you for your insight into slowing down. We are going to look at traveling home to Korea soon and reconnect with family." She comes over, wrapping her arm around my waist.

She's a slight woman, shorter than me even though I'm only five-foot-five.

"I'm happy to help."

"Plus, Ari has been walking around like she won the lottery. I was scared to leave her on her own, but I can see she's ready." Mrs. Choi beams at her daughter, who shifts in place.

I leave them to head home, feeling good about my day. Life feels so positive and I have so much excitement for what's to come with the work changes, life changes, and progressing with Young Jae in our relationship.

Chapter Eighteen

Elise

Dropping onto the couch, I look around our freshly cleaned house. It never takes long to do the weekend reset because we work together over the week to maintain it.

I watch as Young Jae wraps the vacuum cord before heading down the hall. I don't know how I survived a five-year relationship when I was walked all over. I never took myself to be a pushover.

Looking back, I realize that Jake and I started dating a couple of years after my dad and Melanie got married, and he started to pull away. I was grieving the relationship I had lost with my dad and he swooped in on our first date saying all the right things.

He promised me the family I felt I had lost, and now I realize my real family has been here all along.

Young Jae comes in, brushing his hands on his sweats.

"Nothing feels better than having the woman I love helping me create a home in this house." He drops down next to me, lying down with his head on my lap. "You make everything better. I never realized something was missing in this house until you moved in."

Running my hands through his hair, I tease, "Aww, who knew you were such a romantic."

He laughs, because between the two of us, he's the more romantic one and he knows it.

"I was just thinking how even cleaning the house is enjoyable because we do it together." Linking our hands together, I continue to play with his hair.

His eyes close and he hums low in his throat. "That feels nice."

Leaning my head back, I focus on the feel of his hair between my fingers, the weight of his head on my lap. Kimchi lies on my other side, and life feels so good. So complete.

My pocket buzzes, the vibrations not ending. Releasing his hand, I dig my phone out and frown when I see it's my uncle calling. I never hear from him.

"Hello?" My confusion is clear in my voice.

"Elise." His voice isn't friendly, which is odd, seeing as he's never made much effort to get to know me, so there's no reason to be hostile. "I was expecting to hear you're unwell or something. That's the only reason I could think of for you not showing up, but you sound fine to me."

Frowning, my hand pauses on Young Jae's head. "Show up for what?"

"Wow. I never thought you would be so cold. Your dad's funeral. Melaine said you said you were too busy to make it."

My heart stops. My dad's funeral. My throat constricts and my eyes fill with tears. "Excuse me? My dad's dead?" My voice breaks, hand falling to the side as Young Jae bolts up, his hand reaching for mine.

Dead air. That's all I hear, and then, "You didn't know?" His voice is softer now, remorseful.

Tears start to fall and I gasp out, "No. Melanie never called me to tell me. Was he sick? Was it sudden? When did—"

My voice cuts out. Young Jae pulls me onto his lap, stroking my back.

"It was a sudden heart attack, last Tuesday. I'm sorry, Elise. I thought you knew. Melanie said she called you right away and you didn't want to be there." His voice lowers even more, almost sounding ashamed. "I know your relationship has been strained, so I didn't question it."

Scoffing, my tone is sharp as I respond, "It was strained because he constantly let Melanie put a wedge there. I only heard from him on Christmas and my birthday. I don't remember the last time I saw him. But that doesn't mean I would choose to miss his funeral. Choose to opt out of saying goodbye to the man I once looked to as the representation of what a man should be. At least until he decided to distance himself from me because of some bitch he decided to marry."

The words are harsh and normally I would not speak so ill of someone, but I'm tired of holding my tongue when it comes to Melanie.

He apologizes, giving me the information for where my father is buried and the phone number for the lawyer who is handling his will. He says they haven't done the reading yet, but to touch base so I can be there if I choose.

Hanging up, sobs wrack my body. I always imagined that one day I would be able to reconnect with my dad. That he would realize he can have a relationship with his daughter while maintaining his marriage. It didn't need to be either or.

Rage sears through me at the fact Melanie didn't bother to invite me to my father's funeral, a burning feeling right in my chest as I feel hatred for the first time.

Young Jae is silent as he holds me, letting me feel all the feelings instead of trying to cheer me up.

"I can't believe she would refuse me this. The chance to say goodbye. I knew she wasn't a good woman, but I had no idea she would be this cruel. And then to lie about it." Wiping my eyes, I meet Young Jae's gaze. "I always thought we would figure it out one day."

He nods, his expression serious. "It sucks to not get closure, and it's appalling that Melanie would deprive you of the chance for that last goodbye."

"The worst part is, I wouldn't have known if Uncle George hadn't called me. I would've thought he just decided to never answer my calls or reach out even on holidays." Curling into Young Jae, I feel everything drain out of my body. The anger, the sadness, I just feel numb.

His arms tighten around me and I feel his lips in my hair. "Why don't we drive up there this weekend? You can have your moment."

Nodding into his chest, I sigh. "And I guess I should contact the lawyer. Although I can't see any reason to go to that meeting."

"Call first and we can go from there, okay?"

Staying in his arms, I'm so glad he is home to be here with me. He holds me for a bit before I sigh.

Picking up my phone, I dial the number for the lawyer. The conversation is brief, but she encourages me to attend the meeting. I give her my email so she can send the information along.

After the call, Young Jae sets me on the couch, patting my lap so Kimchi comes to cuddle.

"I will be right back, okay?"

Nodding numbly, I pet Kimchi and close my eyes. I can't believe my dad is gone.

Ten minutes later, Young Jae comes downstairs and lifts me into his arms. He carries me into the bedroom and through to the bathroom, where a bubble bath waits with candles lit.

"You relax, process, cry, or whatever you need. I will order in dinner and we can just veg out in any way you want. I will even do mud masks." He kisses me gently on the forehead before leaving and closing the door behind me. Soft music starts to play through the speakers he has wired in nearly every room in the house.

Stripping down, I crawl into the bath and close my eyes. Somehow he managed to figure out what I need without me knowing.

Chapter Nineteen

Elise

Young Jae parks by the gates to the graveyard, shutting the car off and leaving us in silence. I always thought my dad wanted to be cremated, but I guess I really don't—didn't—know him anymore.

My body feels heavy as I sigh and unbuckle. I always regretted not working harder to rebuild my relationship with my dad, but I was so angry with him for letting Melanie drive a wedge between us.

My opening door surprises me. I didn't even notice Young Jae get out of the car. "Thank you."

"Do you want me to come with you?" He rests his hand on the small of my back, pulling me into him.

After a moment, I shake my head. "No. I want to speak my mind and I think it will be easier alone."

His kisses the crown of my head, with a promise he's right here.

Uncle George told me where my dad is buried, so I don't need to spend a lot of time looking.

His gravestone is simple, including his name, date of birth, and date of death. With "Loving Husband" carved into the bottom. Pressing my lips together, I clench my jaw. She didn't even acknowledge me on here.

"Hi, Dad. I never thought the next time I saw you would be like this. But here we are."

I didn't bother reading his obituary. I know it would've been empty of anything truly meaningful. The man he was before he remarried. The man I'm choosing to remember.

"I wish we would've stayed close. I never understood why you pulled away after marrying Melanie. It's not like I ever said anything bad about her. All I wanted was for you to be happy again." Crouching down, my eyes grow blurry. "We were so close, Dad. And it's like that never even mattered."

The tears fall down my cheeks as all the words of hurt and anger fade away. They don't really matter now. Nothing can change in how the time went, how distant we were, or the fact he's gone.

If I learned anything over the past several years, it's that sometimes the most meaningful family is the one you create for yourself.

"I want you to know I'm okay. I don't know if that's important for you. I haven't felt like I mattered much, but maybe somewhere deep inside you still hoped. I have a good life. I've built a family for myself and they're amazing." A wry scoff escapes. "Young Jae and I are together. I know you always liked him. He's everything to me."

Standing, I tuck my hands into my pockets. "I don't really know what else to say. I love you and wish we could've fixed this. It's okay though. Goodbye, Dad."

The air is cool, the breeze holding that fall chill. Shivering, I adjust the collar on my jacket and hurry back to the car. Young Jae is leaning against the vehicle, waiting. I walk right into his arms and lay my head on his chest.

"It doesn't feel like there's a point. We can't rewrite our history and I don't even feel like I know the man anymore. He's not my dad, he's a stranger. It feels empty. Is that horrible to say?" Holding his shirt tight in my hands, I squeeze my eyes shut.

I'm a horrible daughter to say that coming to my father's grave feels empty, but it does. And I can't pretend otherwise, not with Young Jae.

He lifts my chin, brown eyes serious as I meet his gaze. "Hey. It's not horrible. It's simply an unfortunate truth. When was the last time you saw him anyway? Before his wedding, right?"

Nodding. I hadn't even been invited. They "eloped" except her people were there and none of his.

"I think you grieved the loss of your relationship with your father a long time ago. It makes sense that this doesn't feel as impactful." He slides his hand to cup my cheek.

Releasing a heavy sigh, I lean into it. "His gravestone doesn't even say anything about being a father. Like I don't exist."

He presses his forehead to mine. "That would feel awful."

Closing my eyes, I breathe him in. "Honestly, it doesn't even matter. He hasn't acted like a father in years. It hurts, but I think it hurts more that I know he will never show up, asking me to be in his life again. The door is truly closed."

He wraps his arms around me, holding me tight.

After a few minutes, I say, "I guess we better head to the lawyer's. Honestly, I don't know why she wants me there."

Young Jae opens the car door and I slide into the seat. He has the address linked in his GPS and the five-minute drive seems to be over in the blink of an eye.

We're right on time, so the receptionist ushers us into the board room when we enter the building.

When Melanie sees me, her eyes widen in shock. It's the most satisfying part of my day, seeing her open and close her mouth in shock as she tries to figure out how I found out.

Uncle George comes in behind us, his cheeks flushed. "Sorry I'm late." He catches sight of me, he looks a little like my dad when he smiles. "Elise. It's been a long time. I'm happy you came."

Melanie's eyes narrow briefly before she plasters a fake smile on her face. "It's a pleasure, Elise."

Uncle George glares at her but doesn't say anything as the lawyer clears her throat. "Let's get started."

The lawyer, Rose, sits down and pulls out what I'm assuming is dad's will.

"This is the last will and testament of Eric William Cooper, completed in April of this year." She flips the page, but Melanie is making sounds like a dog when they have that weird breathing thing.

"Impossible, we had our wills done after our wedding and nothing has changed since then." Her face is red, and I seriously don't understand what my father saw in her.

"Yes, and he came in this April and updated it, as he did every year." She holds up his file, the thickness evidence of her statement. "Let's proceed." Melanie is quiet at the lawyer's stern tone.

The lawyer reads through the division of Dad's estate. The house, its belongings, and his pension go to Melanie. It's a substantial pension and she looks so self-satisfied. No widow should look that happy over the division of her husband's assets. She starts to arrange her things, thinking it's over.

"To my daughter, Elise Cooper, I leave her mother's engagement ring, being held in trust by my brother, Uncle George." The lawyer reads on.

I freeze. For some reason, I thought Mom's engagement ring was gone. I remember because when Melanie saw a photo of it and declared she wanted the two-carat diamond, he told her it was gone and she didn't talk to him for a week.

Before Melanie can say anything, Rose reads on.

"'I also leave her the savings in an account I set up for her to be provided at the time of my death, in the sum of five hundred thousand dollars at the time of this will, plus any interest it has gained. I have made a lot of mistakes as a father, allowing myself to distance from you. I know that money can't fix anything, but I hope you can use this to build the future and life you want.' I have a letter that he has written to you that he asks you to read when you're ready."

Before I can say anything, Melanie erupts, "This is outrageous! He can't just do that without my knowledge. The money in that account is part of the marital assets."

Everyone in the room stares at her, perhaps seeing a version of her I only suspected for the first time. My father was well-off when they met, and I had wondered if she was marrying him for his money. We all just got our answer.

"Actually, this account was set up prior to your marriage and opened in trust to Elise Cooper. There is no discourse on whether this is yours or not, the will, as well as the account documentation, are binding," the lawyer states coolly.

Young Jae holds my hand tightly as Melanie looks at me, pure hatred in her eyes. "You had to go and show up, didn't you?"

Before I can respond, the lawyer tells her that whether or not I'm here, the will would still stand.

"I would like to conclude the reading of the will. So please, hold your questions until the end." Rose's tone is cold as she stares at Melanie.

Her lips clamp down as she seethes in silence while the lawyer concludes with a few other small accounts. It's apparent Melanie had no idea they existed as her face contorts with each one. My father designates money to a few charities, including the animal shelter in Willowbrook Lake. He wants the donations to be made in the name of his late wife, Anna Cooper. Hearing my mom's name instead of Melanie's makes my lips quirk up a little.

"This concludes the reading of the will. If anyone has any ques—"

"I do not agree with this. He was not in his right mind! There must be something I can do." She glares at me. "The best thing I ever did was push him to cut you out. You stupid little cun—"

Rose cuts her off, her voice hard as she glares at Melanie. "I will not accept any sort of display of animosity or threat. Mr. Cooper was well in his right mind. And you may want to carefully consider what you say in this room. The paperwork to start the transition of assets is at the front. Please see yourself out and return the forms to us as quickly as possible. If you approach myself, my staff, or anyone else pertaining to this will with anything but a calm and respectful attitude, I will see that the division of your assets is drawn out personally."

Melanie leaves in a huff, and no one else in the room follows her.

Uncle George looks at me, remorse in his eyes. "I wish I had known how she was. I would have tried to knock sense into my brother."

He pulls a ring box out of his coat pocket, handing it to me.

Opening it, I stare at the ring I've only seen in photos.

"I know I'm probably too late, but I would love to reconnect and rebuild a relationship. I'm sorry I haven't been there." He stands, his hands gesturing aimlessly as if he doesn't know what to do with them.

Pushing out of the chair, I give him a hug. "It's never too late."

Young Jae gives us some privacy, going to speak to the paralegal and gathering the documents I need to fill out.

After saying goodbye to my uncle, with a promise to visit at Thanksgiving, Young Jae and I head to the car.

As we settle in, he whistles. "Well, that was something else."

Blowing out air, I shake myself a little. "Never did I expect any of that. Well, maybe Melanie's behavior."

We laugh, the sound weird after everything that has happened.

Young Jae turns on the seat warmer for me and we start the journey home.

"Are you going to read the letter?" he asks, reaching over to hold my hand.

Licking my lips, I stare at the manila folder in my lap. "One day."

He squeezes.

"What about that savings? You could do almost anything you want with that. Add on to Perk Up. Explore the world." His thumb strokes my hand as I ponder his question. He doesn't press me and I know he's asking out of curiosity and not because the money means anything to him.

"I don't know. I guess leave it invested for now and sit with it. My life doesn't have to change because of it, so I don't want to be rash." I smile at him, still a little in shock about the money and the ring. "Hey, do you have a safe or something I can put this in? I can't see myself wearing it right now, and I want to keep it safe."

He smiles at me. "Of course. I have a safe and I will give you the combination."

"Thank you for being with me today. I love you."

"I love you too."

We're quiet, my eyes growing heavy as the day fully catches up to me. Young Jae turns on the music as my head starts to bob, lifting my hand to kiss it as sleep takes me.

Chapter Twenty

Young Jae

Owen washes his hands before joining me at the table. He's been working steadily on the closet and it should be done by the end of the day.

"I don't know how you managed to hold it together. I may have tackled that woman." He shakes his head, eyes blazing.

I just filled him in on what happened at the meeting with the lawyer. Elise has been quiet the past week since going, taking her time to process. It's hard seeing her so withdrawn when she's normally such a happy person.

"Trust me, if I wasn't holding Elise's hand, I probably would've done something to get kicked out. Watching her face as the lawyer read out everything being left to Elise was hilarious. I suspect the initial will she had him draw up when they were together didn't list any of that." At least she no longer has any reason to reach out to Elise.

Serving myself some pasta, I pass the bowl to Owen. We're silent for a bit, both in our own heads as we eat.

"Adeline is a little worried about her. She said she's been pretty quiet in their group chat." Owen looks up at me, searching my expression.

Sighing, I set my fork down and lean back. "Here too. I've been trying to give her space to sort through her feelings, but I do plan on talking to her. I've got her."

"I know you do. That's what I told Adeline. She just worries, she knows what it's like having horrible people try to manipulate and dictate." Owen taps on the table. "Do you think that wife of his will show up in town? Try to intimidate Elise into giving up what her father left her?"

Shaking my head, I scoff. "No. She doesn't seem like the type to get her hands dirty. Besides, she wasn't left destitute. She's probably living the high life trying to find her next wealthy husband."

He grunts in disgust. A sentiment I second.

It boggles my mind that someone would keep a child from their parent's funeral, adult or not. The days since then have been quiet. Elise comes home from work, we eat dinner and she cleans up, then she cuddles me on the couch until it's time for bed. We've talked a little, but not the way we normally do. It's been hard, but she needs me to be a quiet presence and that's what I will do.

We finish eating in silence, both of our minds occupied before he heads back upstairs with a promise to be done by the end of the day and an offer to help rally around Elise if we need.

Owen finishes the closet just as Elise is walking in the door. Kimchi greets her like normal, bouncing around and wriggling, waiting for the cue to come forward. Elise bends down, her smile looking a little more genuine today. She picks Kimchi up, holding her close.

"Just in time, Owen was going to show me our new closet." I gesture for her to go first.

She sets Kimchi down, surprise crossing her face. "It's done already?"

"That's what happens when you hire the best." He smirks, leading the way into the primary bedroom. "I will stay and help Young Jae move the furniture back to its space, but I vacuumed, mopped, and dusted everything too."

Elise stares, stunned. "Wow. You really didn't have to do that."

She goes into the walk-in closet, which has doubled in size, before coming back out, her eyes wide. "This is bigger than I thought. It's the closet of dreams. We literally don't need a dresser anymore."

Owen points past her to the hamper storage. "I built the closet around the hampers so they're not cumbersome. This way they have a home and blend in with the rest of the storage."

Elise opens the drawers, exploring while Owen and I move the furniture back into the room, except the dresser. We decide to pop that into the empty bedroom at the end of the hall for now.

As we finish, Elise starts moving our clothes out of the guest closet into our refinished one.

"Do you care how your things are organized?" Her voice is excited and her eyes shine with excitement, so I shake my head.

"Have at it. I'm going to order us a pizza, I hope you don't mind." Owen follows me out and I can't stop the grin that forms. "Who knew it would take a closet to get her to cheer up?"

Owen stares at me, brows lifted. "Why do you think I worked so hard to finish it today? Nothing helps more than something else to occupy your energy. She will be able to think through what she's working, but it won't be the only thing she's focused on. It usually helps me, so I thought it might work for Elise too."

"Thanks, man. Want to stay for pizza?" I pull up the number for Cliff's.

"Nah, Adeline is making some new recipe and she invited my mom over to celebrate. Mom found a place and is moving in a few weeks." He rests his hand on my shoulder, squeezing. "I'm glad that you have Elise the way you've always been meant to. And I'm glad she finally has a man who cherishes her the way she should."

He heads out, muttering something about becoming too damn soft. Grinning, I quickly order the pizza before heading back upstairs.

I find Elise sitting on the floor, surrounded by clothes. Her lips move silently as she points at the different areas of the closet.

"How's it going in here?" I sit next to her, picking up a shirt I forgot I had.

She smiles. "Good. Honestly, this is what I needed. I haven't been able to shake all the conflicting emotions from finding out my dad passed, missing his funeral, and then the influx of information at the meeting. Thank you for just being with me and tolerating my moodiness."

Shifting closer to her, I wrap my arm around her waist. "No need to thank me. It's the least I could do."

"I think I was mostly processing the fact that Dad really updated his will behind Melanie's back to include me. I don't know what his life was like, but maybe there was more I didn't see, and he was trying to protect me in some weird way. At least, that's how I'm choosing to see it." She rests her head on my shoulder.

"That could be. Especially seeing the person Melanie actually is." Rubbing my hand up and down her arm, I smile when she wraps her arms around me.

"I feel like I have closure. I'm not ready to read the letter he wrote to me, but maybe one day." She sighs, pulling away from me. "Now, let's get this all put away before the pizza arrives. I'm starving."

Chapter Twenty-One

Elise

Popping the pies into the oven, I set the timer before moving on to prep the sunflower bread recipe I want to test out. Along with adding the hot menu items to the menu, I have completely revamped the sandwich menu during the day to be more gourmet.

My stomach turns when I crack the egg and add it to the mix, a wave of nausea passing through me. "I better not be getting sick again," I mutter.

Digging through the drawers, I grab a mask from the box I keep and put it on. The last thing I need is to get anyone sick and destroy all the growth I've made. My inspection grades have always been perfect and I intend to keep them that way.

I hear Mary in the front, her chipper voice greeting another customer. We've gotten so busy, I have posted an ad to hire a part-time employee to help during rush hours.

Covering the bread, I leave it to rise and wash up, joining Mary up front.

I snag a banana muffin and start nibbling at it, the nausea passing. I glance at the clock and realize it's been almost six hours since I've eaten. No wonder I feel sick.

"Elise, this is my daughter, Morgan." Mary gestures to a pretty brunette who looks exactly how I imagine Mary did at the same age.

"It's so nice to meet you. I've heard so much about you." I smile at her.

Her responding grin is friendly. "I'm sure only some of it is true."

Mary gives an offended gasp. "I don't lie, and I never need to lie about you. Now, how are things going? Are your coworkers warming up to you?"

Morgan shrugs. "I guess. Now that the school year has started, we're all so busy that there's no time to notice that I'm not invited out with the rest of them. Anyway, I spend most of my time on the farm."

"Morgan is renting a small house on a farm. The farmer, Nathan, is a quiet sort. Seems a bit shy. He's a fair bit older than you too, isn't he?" Mary asks, turning to make a chai latte.

Morgan smiles a little. "I guess. He's thirty-nine."

"So twelve years. I guess it's not like he's twenty years older and renting to a young woman. Just make sure he treats you with respect." Mary turns, handing Morgan the drink.

"Of course, Momma." Morgan takes it, smiling indulgently. "Anyway, I just felt like getting out, so I figured I would pop in. We should go get pedicures one day."

Taking another bite of my banana muffin, I watch as Mary rounds the counter to give her daughter a hug. It warms my heart to see such a close mother-daughter bond. I wonder if that's how my relationship with my own mom would've been had she not passed. "Sounds good. Let me know when."

"It was nice to meet you, Elise." She waves and leaves with her drink.

Mary sighs. "Being a parent never gets any easier. I can see how lonely she is and there's nothing I can do about it."

"You're doing everything you need to. You're there for her when she needs you." Covering my mouth, I fight off a yawn.

Mary's eyes narrow on me. "You've been yawning all day. You okay?"

Turning, I toss the wrapper from the muffin into the garbage. "Yeah, I think I'm just fighting something. I'm going to go home and go to bed. The sunflower bread is rising. And—oh my god! The pies."

Rushing into the kitchen, I open the oven and pull them out. My shoulders drop when I see they're perfect.

"Go home. Rest. I will finish the bread," Mary shoos me out, her mom voice brooking no room for argument.

Young Jae isn't home when I get there since it's so early, so I let Kimchi outside before calling her to bed for a nap.

When I wake up, it's dark and Young Jae is sitting on the edge of the bed rubbing my back.

"What time is it?" Rubbing my eyes, I feel super groggy.

"It's seven. Dinner is ready and I already cleaned the kitchen. I went into Perk Up earlier and Mary said you were exhausted all day. Are you feeling better?" He helps me sit up, handing me a glass of water.

Stretching my neck, I feel sluggish and still exhausted. "Not really. I think I'm going to come right back to bed after dinner."

"Good idea. I just made a simple meal. Roasted chicken breast, asparagus, and some fried rice." He stands, holding his hand out for mine.

Taking his hand, I stand and follow him out of the room. "It smells delicious."

I feel his eyes on me throughout dinner, even though I try to be fully engaged in the conversation. Despite my hopes, dinner doesn't help me with my energy, so I kiss him and head back to bed, my eyes closing before I finish laying down.

***

The next morning I wake up feeling fresh and perky. Young Jae isn't in bed, which is unusual considering the early morning.

I wash up and get ready for the day before heading downstairs. I find Young Jae in the kitchen making breakfast burritos.

"You seem well-rested." He smiles as he hands me a plate. "I thought I would make breakfast in case you wanted to rest a little longer."

Kissing him on the cheek, I take the plate. "Thank you. I do feel much better, I guess I just needed a solid night's sleep. What do you have going on today?"

"Thistle Creek just sent me updated info on the grain elevator, so just a continuation of that project." He dives into details of what he's working on and I love seeing his passion. The creation of something new while also maintaining a piece of history. I can tell that he loves this more than just creating something new.

"I can't wait to visit it when it's done." I finish breakfast and sip my coffee.

He laughs. "Same, but that's a couple years down the road. Even though we're not rebuilding, a lot of internal structure needs to be developed."

"I still can't wait. Will there be an opening gala? Something I can dress up for and be arm candy when you go as the amazing architect that designed the space?" Young Jae is it for me, I know in one, two, three years we will still be together.

His eyes soften as he looks at me. "I'm sure there will at least be a grand opening we could attend."

With a bounce in my step, I clean up breakfast, kiss him, and head to Perk Up to open. I have a couple interviews today and I want to get the prep done early.

By the time Mary comes in at noon, I've concluded the interviews and the lunch rush has started. I don't know if it was the process of screening potential employees or the busier than normal opening rush, but I'm exhausted again.

Mary takes over at the counter so I can restock the sandwiches and other prepared foods. She typically cooks the hot meals in the evenings, my preference the baking and daytime foods that I can prepare somewhat in advance.

My head starts to feel woozy as I finish a roast chicken on focaccia with guacamole, bacon, and green leaf lettuce. Bracing my hands on the counter, I clench my eyes as a wave of dizziness hits me. What is going on? I felt fine this morning.

It passes as quickly as it came, so I finish in the back and restock the case at the counter. Every day we nearly clear out and I haven't had as much to bring to the seniors home. Making a mental note, I plan to make extra so I can continue to bring treats at least three times a week.

The lunch rush ends, leaving Mary and me to clean up.

"I'm going to tackle the patio. I think I need some fresh air." I wave my hand in front of my face. The room feels hot and it's making me nauseous.

"Are you okay?" Mary's face is concerned.

"Yeah, I'm okay." I head outside and clean up the tables, wiping the surfaces and straightening chairs. Once it's all cleaned, I sit down and enjoy the gentle breeze blowing.

The door to Perk Up opens, Mary coming out with a couple mugs. "I made you some tea."

Taking it gratefully, I sip and enjoy feeling my head clear a bit.

We sit in silence for a bit, enjoying the cooler breeze of fall. The leaves are starting to change and as much as I love summer, this time of year is my favorite.

Mary clears her throat, angling herself to look at me. "I'm worried about you, Elise. You're paler than normal, your energy is low, and I've noticed the dizzy spells and nausea. I think you should go see a doctor. None of that is normal, especially for you."

Setting my mug down, I face her. "Mary, I'm fine."

"Look, I know I'm your employee and nothing more—" she starts but I cut her off.

"You know you're more than an employee to me, Mary. You're a friend too."

She smiles, patting my arm. "Thank you, hon. Then as your friend, I am asking you to go see a doctor before this becomes more serious."

Her concern means a lot to me, especially since some days she feels like the mom I missed out on since mine passed when I was only four. Sighing, I concede. "Okay, I will call and make an appointment. But for today, I need your help deciding which of these candidates are the best fit. They all interviewed well."

Mary stands, happy with my agreement to see a doctor, and we head back inside to look at their resumes and the notes I made after the interview concluded. It takes some back and forth, but we finally agree that Nicole is the best fit. She had the best overall interview, is eager to learn about more than just the front end stuff, and out of them all, I feel like her personality will mesh with Mary and me the best.

I excuse myself to my little back office and make the call. She eagerly accepts the job and I schedule her to start the following week. Hanging up, I lean back in my chair and close my eyes. Mary is right I need to call the doctor. I've never been this exhausted in my life.

"Elise? Are you okay?"

Opening my eyes to the concern in Mary's voice, I yawn. "Yeah, sorry. After speaking to Nicole, I figured I would close my eyes for a minute."

Her brows furrow. "You've been back here for forty-five minutes. Adeline and Rae are out front asking for you."

Inhaling sharply, I glance at the time. Damn. I've never done that before. "Yeah. Okay. Tell them I will be out in five—I'm going to call my doctor and set up that appointment."

Chapter Twenty-Two

Elise

One of the best things about living in a small town is that there's usually not much of a wait to see the doctor. The downside is, when you go to the office, you probably know the majority of the people waiting to see said doctor.

The nurse asked if I was okay switching to the new doctor, Dr. Wright. When she heard what was bothering me, she thought I should get in right away, but Dr. Stevens wouldn't be available until early next week.

Hudson Wright has been in town for maybe a few weeks and was the gossip of the town. Relieving me and Young Jae. From what I've heard, he's been very accommodating, so I eagerly switched away from Dr. Stevens. Despite being an excellent doctor, she's a bit gruff and better suited for the older patients.

Several people approach me while waiting to be called, asking if I'm okay. Assuring them I'm fine doesn't seem to alleviate the concern, so I try to shift the focus. "Did you see the progress on the new autobody shop? It seems like the guys are doing a great job."

The chatter shifts to Liam, another new man in town and I lean back, satisfied as they start gossiping about him. Mostly trying to figure out who he should marry.

"Elise Cooper?" a deep voice calls for me.

Turning, I see Hudson Wright for the first time. It makes sense why he's the topic of chatter. Tall, dark hair with a hint of gray appearing, he is an attractive man.

Standing, I wave at the crowd, but they hardly notice.

"I see what you did there. I will have to take notes." His voice is full of humor, which I meet with a grin.

"You don't grow up in a small town without learning some tricks."

I follow him into an exam room, where I proceed to fill him in on what's been going on. He listens, taking notes on the computer.

"I think we will start with some bloodwork. I'm sending it over now and they will fit you in right away. Then come back tomorrow afternoon and I will have the results. It's the best place to start." He finishes typing before turning to look at me.

Appreciating how quick he is, I follow and head next door to get my blood drawn. It doesn't take long and soon I'm home, on the couch, with Kimchi curled between my legs. I pick up the new book I'm reading and settle in for a lazy afternoon.

I wake up to Young Jae crouched in front of me, pulling my book off my face. "You okay?"

Tucking my hair behind my ears as I sit up, careful not to disturb Kimchi. I clear my throat. "Yeah, I'm good. I went to the doctor today and got some bloodwork done to check my levels. Maybe I'm low in iron or something, making me tired."

He doesn't look convinced that would be causing my sudden exhaustion, but if I dwell too long, I can't help but think of my mother's cancer diagnosis. I don't remember a lot about her, but I do remember she was tired a lot.

"Yeah, maybe. Dinner will be a quick and easy ramen tonight. I was in a ton of meetings all day and I think maybe we both need a night of vegging on the couch." He kisses me, before letting Kimchi outside.

Stretching, I stand up and join him in the kitchen. "Sounds good."

I grab everything I need to make lemonade, craving the citrusy goodness. "The new doctor is nice. Maybe we should introduce him to Ari?"

Young Jae laughs. "Ari said she would die alone rather than date someone who looks at other women's 'hoo ha's' for a living. So I think family doctor makes that list."

Chuckling, I respond, "I can absolutely see her saying something like that. He's probably a little too old for her anyway, I would guess he's around forty."

I finish the lemonade, pouring myself and Young Jae a glass and take a sip. Groaning, I look at him. "I don't think lemonade has ever tasted this damn good."

He grins wolfishly, his eyes heated. "I thought that sound was reserved for me."

Meeting his gaze, I take another sip and moan teasingly. "Maybe later, when you earn it."

I sashay away to let Kimchi in the house and feed her dinner before sitting on the couch, setting our lemonades on the coffee table. Young Jae comes in, bringing the ramen and handing a bowl to me.

"What do you want to watch?" He turns on the TV.

"You pick, it's your turn." My stomach rumbles, so while he searches, I start eating. The spicy broth hits the spot, and by the time he finds some cop show, I'm done eating.

He gapes at me. "I don't think I've ever seen you eat that fast. There's more on the stove, I made a couple packs."

Excited, I head into the kitchen to serve myself some more, glad my stomach seems to be enjoying the ramen. It's been a little hard to eat the past few days, not everything agreeing with me. I must have some bug, which is why I don't think the bloodwork will come up with anything except maybe a high white blood cell count.

Rejoining Young Jae on the couch, we watch the show and to my surprise I really like it. Cop shows aren't usually my go-to, but this one has a good mix of humor and drama, with maybe a little romance mixed in.

I finish my second bowl, finally full. Patting my stomach, I say, "That really hit the spot. Some days you just need a good ramen reset."

We snuggle on the couch, watching the show, and at some point, I must fall asleep again because I wake up to Young Jae carrying me to bed.

"Damn, again. I must be getting sick. Thank you for carrying me," I mumble, kissing his neck.

His eyes are concerned, but he gives me a small smile. "Anytime. Just make sure you go back to the doctor tomorrow to ensure everything is okay."

With a promise to do that, I curl up and go to sleep convinced tomorrow won't bring any news I don't already know.

Chapter Twenty-Three

Elise

"You're pregnant." Dr. Wright's voice is gentle as he delivers a blow I wasn't expecting.

"Not possible, I have an IUD. I had my typical light period like two or three weeks ago," I stammer, positive it's wrong. Or the clinic got it mixed up.

I sit there, waiting for him to agree. Waiting for some chance that this is wrong.

Time stands still and the look of empathy on his face feels like a punch in the gut.

"Unfortunately, IUDs still have a one percent failure rate."

No, no, no. Kids aren't a part of my plan anymore and they're certainly not a part of Young Jae's plan. Is this it? Do I need to decide between termination, something I don't believe in for myself, or my relationship. Sure, I'm all about choosing, but not making Young Jae wear a condom because I have this stupid, failing IUD is my fault not the baby's.

"I see." My words are barely a whisper.

I listen almost as if in a vacuum as he goes over my options before stepping out to give me a minute to process. I could take some time, but it would need to be soon. I have to start taking prenatal vitamins. I need to get this dumb IUD out. I need to prepare myself to accept that my life is about to change in a way I never wanted it to.

And worst of all, I can't even talk to anyone about it. Adeline and Rae want children so badly, but neither can get pregnant. And here I am, a one percent chance of getting pregnant and there's a baby. Just growing inside me.

My heart races as I think about Young Jae. He's not going to be happy. He was adamant about no children. Gripping the edges of the chair I'm sitting on, all the symptoms start to make sense. How was I so blind?

The door opens and Dr. Wright comes back in. "I can fit you in any day this week or next to do the next steps. You don't need to decide now."

Clearing my throat, I shake my head. "It's not a choice. I won't terminate." My voice is hoarse, quiet.

"Okay. I will get everything set up to remove the IUD. And I will send off a requisition to get an ultrasound so we can get a date. I will be right back."

Nodding numbly, I panic, "Wait! Can you send the requisition to Thistle Creek or Mistik Ridge? I'm not ready to share the news yet and this town loves its gossip."

He agrees, then leaves to go get whatever he needs.

Less than thirty minutes later, I have no IUD and I'm on the road to Mistik Ridge. They had a cancellation and were able to fit me in.

Stopping at the drugstore, I pick up prenatal vitamins and stuff them into the bottom of my purse. Setting a reminder on my phone.

No one recognizes me as I park outside the clinic and go inside, where I'm ushered into a room right away.

I watch as the tech preps everything. When I go to lift my shirt, she shakes her head. "Based on the doctor's hypothesis for when you had implantation bleeding, we need to check inside."

I feel like I'm having an out-of-body experience. I watch as she shows me on the screen the little bean that will grow into a baby.

Seeing the little speck that will grow into a human being is surreal. Part of me still thought this wasn't real. It's sinking in now that I will be a mother in less than nine months.

As much as I was on board having no kids, seeing the little form does something to me. Tears well and I watch the screen, feeling a little more okay with whatever comes.

After we're done, she suggests I wait as the radiologist is able to look at the scan now and give me an approximate of how far along I am.

The next hour passes by so slowly, but by the time I leave, I know I'm about five weeks along and due at the beginning of May.

I take the long way home, still processing everything. Somehow, I need to keep Young Jae in the dark until I've had enough time to accept this because I can't process a baby and the possibility of him asking me to terminate or ending the relationship. I can't imagine him doing something so cold, but I also know he doesn't want this.

Our lives are going to change forever and I'm taking away his choice in the matter. I know I would be upset too.

My phone rings, the Bluetooth loud in my car. Glancing at the screen, I'm relieved when I see it's Uncle George instead of Young Jae. I need more time to collect myself before I see Young Jae or he will know something is up.

"Hi, Uncle George," I greet him, my voice cheery. It's easy enough. Customer service has helped me perfect the happy, everything is great voice.

"Hey. I wanted to check in. The reading of the will was a lot." His voice is gentle, but a little cautious.

We've texted a bit since that day, but I think he's trying to let me take the wheel on building a relationship. At least that's my best guess from what little I know about him.

"It was, but I'm okay. It helps me to know that even though we drifted apart, he still thought about me and wanted to take care of me." My voice is softer, more real.

He grunts. "I wish I had known how bad it was. I would've stepped in. She always rubbed me the wrong way, but he seemed happy. I should've known better when he stopped seeing you."

The regret in his voice is thick. It's easy enough to overlook things when you think someone is happy. I know how easy it is to pretend everything is okay when it's not.

"The only one capable of changing anything was Dad. I don't think he knew how to ask for help. I felt so hurt by his distance that I pulled away, too, even though I could've pushed my way back in. But we all can look at what we could've done and sit in regret. It doesn't change anything." Breathing out a sigh, I rub my hand over my head.

I hope that I can look at things this clearly when it comes to the baby, but the distraction right now is welcome.

We talk for a while longer, making plans to meet sometime in the holiday season. When we hang up, I feel like a connection to my dad is coming back and even though I can never rebuild what he and I lost, I can rebuild with Uncle George.

By the time I park in the garage, it's past seven. Young Jae has called a few times, but I let it go to voicemail.

He greets me as I come in the door, his expression worried. "You didn't answer my call. Is everything okay?"

Removing my shoes, I walk into his arms and hug him tight. "Yeah, everything is fine. Nothing serious is wrong with me, I just need to take some vitamins."

It's not a total lie. It's a lie by omission, but I can't tell him now. Not yet.

"Well, I made a really delicious dinner and I thought we could take the paddleboards out tonight. Enjoy the water before it gets too cold." He leads me to the table where a lovely dinner is waiting. Chicken, roast veggies, and sweet potato fries ready and plated, with a fresh bouquet of dahlias in a vase to the side.

Trying not to let him see through my calm exterior, I tease, "You know you don't have to bribe me with tasty food and a spontaneous date night to get sex, right? It's usually guaranteed."

He laughs. "Good to know."

We eat, and I let him lead the conversation until it feels effortless, the pregnancy somehow moving to the back of my mind. It's still early on, we have a lot of time to adjust and reframe our future.

We cleanup together before loading up our paddleboards. We bought Kimchi a life preserver and have started bringing her along with us. She took to it right away, but as Young Jae secures her to his board, part of me is envious.

"What do you think about adopting another dog one day?" I push off, paddling on the calm water. The sun is warm, but the light breeze is cool.

Young Jae paddles up alongside me, Kimchi sitting with her eyes half closed. "I have been thinking about it and think it's a great idea. We should go to the shelter on Sunday and visit the dogs."

Laughing, I ignore the guilt in my chest. "We can look, but I want something similar in size to Kimchi. It's probably too much to hope we could rescue another Jack Russell. Let's not rush, I was just putting it out there."

He gives me a sneaky look. "You never know when the right one will appear. I can't make any guarantees I won't come home with a dog one day now that I know you're open to it."

Laughing, I resist the urge to rub my stomach. It's probably more welcome than the surprise I have for him.

We finish paddleboarding and head home. Now that I know why I'm not feeling well, I sneak some saltines as he takes a quick shower. A quick online search gives me some ideas of how to help with the nausea, but there's not much to do about the exhaustion. Just a lot of articles saying it should pass by week thirteen.

"Joy," I mutter, closing the search as Young Jae comes downstairs.

We settle in on the couch, both picking up our books to read. He massages my feet with one hand as he reads, always taking care of me.

I pick up my phone, opening my group chat with Adeline and Rae, but I can't bring myself to tell them the news. It's going to break their hearts and I feel like I will be rubbing it in their faces that I'm pregnant. I can't imagine being in their shoes, wanting something so much and it not happening, only to find out someone who doesn't even want that is getting it.

I know they will be happy for me, because they're that great of friends, but I think I would struggle to find joy in the situation.

It sucks to feel alone in this, but everyone I would normally talk to about this would be too hard to tell.

Chapter Twenty-Four

Elise

It comes to me as I head out of Perk Up for the day. Brynne. She's the perfect person to talk to and I know Adeline isn't working today.

Instead of going home, I text Young Jae really quick that I'm going to run a couple of errands. Starting my car, I head toward Willowbrook Lake Animal Shelter. The parking lot is empty, which is both a relief and sad.

Brynne comes from the back as I enter, the bell announcing my arrival.

"Elise, what a surprise." She smiles, curious.

"I was hoping to cuddle a dog and talk to you about something." Wringing my hands together, I try to ignore my nerves.

She looks at me, her eyes piercing, before she nods. "I know just the dog. If you want to go to one of the meet and greet rooms, I will go get her and meet you there. Room four, please. It has the newest couches."

Finding it, I sit on the loveseat and wait. Brynne comes in with a tiny dog. Smaller than Kimchi. Which surprises me because the majority of dogs that end up in the shelter are larger breeds.

"This is Pepper. She's some kind of schnauzer cross. She's only five weeks old. Her mom and the rest of the litter were deceased when she was found. She was in rough shape, which is why she's so small." Brynne hands me Pepper, who lays in my lap and goes right to sleep.

My eyes fill with tears and I start crying. Petting her softly, I grieve over her lost family. "Oh my gosh. I'm so sorry. I can't help the tears, it's—well, it's the hormones."

Brynne narrows her eyes on me before my words sink in. "You're pregnant?"

Tears continue to fall as I nod. "No one knows. I just found out yesterday and I'm still processing. I haven't told anyone and I just need to talk it out."

"I'm happy to listen, but why me?" She watches as I reverently pet Pepper, cooing at her as I try to think of the best way to explain why without offending her.

Sighing, I admit, "I know you're a vault. Adeline and Rae would be supportive, but pregnancy is a tender subject. And Young Jae—well, he doesn't want kids. So I'm trying to wrap my head around this before I tell him and completely erupt his life."

She cringes for me. "Yeah, that's tough. How are you feeling about it?"

The silence as she waits for my response is heavy, but I haven't taken the time to think of myself in this situation outside of how it will impact my relationship and friendships.

"I was always neutral about kids, but when Dr. Wright asked about termination, it wasn't even a possibility. I think if I let myself, I'm excited about it. The idea that with Young Jae, we've created this life, a combination of the two of us, makes me happy. Even though at first I admit I was regretful and was hoping it was wrong." The words are true. If I allow myself to see past what I worry everyone else will think, happiness is there.

She smiles softly. "Don't you think there's a possibility that Young Jae will feel the same?"

Shrugging, I gently stroke Pepper over her tiny head. "There's a possibility. But he may also look at it as a betrayal."

She scoffs. "I'm sorry, did you get pregnant on purpose? Were you the only one having sex? He's not that pigheaded. He may be as shocked as you, but you won't know his reaction until you give him the chance."

Brynne is right. I need to tell him, give him the chance to process and see what happens. Picking up Pepper, I snuggle her a little closer. "Man, you're adorable. I wish I could stay longer, but I have something I need to do."

Handing Pepper back to Brynne, I'm sad to leave her behind, but one baby at a time.

"Good luck. If you need anything, I'm around." She holds Pepper close and it hurts to walk away from the puppy, but there are still too many unknowns.

"Thank you, Brynne." Taking a deep breath, I head to my car and head home.

Young Jae is in the kitchen when I arrive. He's talking to someone on the phone, so I head to the couch and pull out my laptop. Searching for tips to help during the first trimester, I scroll through a few articles.

Young Jae is still chatting away, and from the conversation, it sounds like it's Ji Hoon. This could take a while. Shifting, my jeans digging into my stomach, I stand and head upstairs to change. I definitely feel like my head isn't fully focused, almost like there's a haze hovering. The exhaustion every day seems to take over.

I finish changing and quickly pull my hair back into a braid before heading back downstairs. As I come around the corner, I see Young Jae sitting on the couch, a plate of nachos in his hand, but his eyes are on my computer screen.

"Are you pregnant?" His voice is rough, his eyes wide. He reminds me of a horse that's seen or heard something in the bushes.

Lifting my hands up, I speak in a low tone. But I can't help the tremble that wavers. "Yes. I just found out yesterday. It's why I've been so unwell."

He sets the plate down, his brows shooting up. "You've known for over twenty-four hours?"

Stepping a little closer, I put my hands on my stomach. Young Jae tracks the movement, creases forming between his brows. "Yes, I—"

"And when were you going to tell me?" His voice is low, measured. Young Jae doesn't yell, even when he's pissed, and I know he's not happy.

Tears forming, I look up at the ceiling to fight them back. I wasn't happy either. I'm still not sure where on the line I stand, but I'm leaning toward the acceptance and happy side of things.

"I was trying to process the news. It came as a shock to me, and I wanted to know I could handle your reaction too." I move to the couch, sitting on the edge, close to him but not touching. "I wasn't planning on you finding out this way. I was going to tell you over dinner."

He rubs his hands on his sweats before dropping his head back. "What is it, like a one percent chance?"

It's hard to keep the wryness from my voice. "That's what the doctor told me."

I sit there quietly while he processes is one of the hardest things I will ever have to do. He's muttering to himself in Korean but speaking too low and fast for me to translate in my head.

"What are you going to do?" he asks, but he already knows the answer.

"I had my IUD taken out and started on prenatal vitamins last night." Standing, I go to my purse and grab the picture from my ultrasound. Setting it on the couch between us, I take a deep breath. With a sigh, I say, "I'm about five weeks along. The baby will be here at the beginning of May."

He lifts his head, not meeting my eyes as he picks up the photo. They marked where the baby is. He stares at it for a moment before looking at my stomach and then meeting my gaze. His expression is unreadable, which is a new experience for me.

Remembering what Brynne said about giving him a chance, I rush to clear everything off my chest before he has a chance to unload what's going on in his head.

"I know this isn't what you want. It wasn't what I wanted either. I was more than happy to spend my life with you, childfree. But I also won't terminate the pregnancy. I'm sorry for taking away any part of that decision, but I won't force you—"

YoungJae is beside me, his hand gripping mine before I finish. "Elise, there is no journey I won't go on with you. Did I see babies in my future? No, I didn't. But your baby. *Our* baby. I'm on board. I'm surprised. And more than a little shocked. Sometimes things happen and if this baby was created on one percent odds, then who are we to say it wasn't meant to be."

I start bawling right there, all the emotions, stress, relief, and hormones combining into one weeping, snotty mess. Young Jae stares in shock for a moment, I'm not a huge crier, before leaping into action. He grabs a tissue and starts wiping my face.

Shushing me, he holds me in his arms until the tears slow.

"And now we can't get Pepper!" Remembering the little dog, I start crying even more.

"What? Who's Pepper?"

"The little puppy I held when I told Brynne I was pregnant because I had no one to talk to, and she's so little and so cute, but we're having a baby, and we already have one dog, but I love her so much." I'm wailing now, the tears uncontrollable.

He holds me close, rubbing my back. When my tears finally subside, he lifts me and settles me onto his lap. "Okay, let's put a pin in the puppy thing. Why do you feel like you couldn't talk to anyone? I guess I understand the need to process it before telling me. But what about Adeline and Rae. They've been there for you no matter what."

Wringing my hands, fresh tears fall. "They both want kids so bad and can't have them. And then here I am, Miss Fertile Myrtle, pregnant by accident."

He chuckles.

My head drops. "I feel so awful that I get what they want when I didn't even plan it or want it."

Young Jae strokes his hands up and down my arms, lips pursed as he thinks about my anxieties.

"They may have mixed emotions because of their own experiences, but they would be happy for you and for us. Their own experiences don't invalidate yours, and they're not the type of women who would ever make you feel bad about this. It may make them sad because of what they're going through, but not because they aren't happy for you." He holds my gaze, his eyes intense on mine. "Two things can be true at once, and it's okay. But they're your closest friends and they would want to know this news."

Slumping down, I feel the weight lifted by his words. "I think I messed up the entire pregnancy announcement thing. Let's invite them all over next Sunday and tell them the news. Right now, let's just acclimate to the news and figure out how to deal with how exhausted I am."

He kisses me deeply. "Well, the best way to start is by eating comfort food. The nachos might need a refresh. I will pop them into the oven for a few minutes. Why don't you find something to watch."

He stands, pausing when I grab his wrist. "I love you. And this baby is going to be so damn cute, neither of us will ever remember a day we didn't want it."

Bending to brush his lips against mine, he smiles. "Damn straight. I love you too."

Chapter Twenty-Five

Young Jae

The animal shelter is busy for a Saturday and I hope Pepper is still there. I heard Elise crying over her again last night and she only met the dog a few days ago.

The doors are propped open, a couple in front of me asking about small dogs. Brynne is at the counter, but she sends them back to where Adeline must be working.

When she sees me, she grins. "Let me guess, Pepper?"

Laughing, I stride to the counter. "How'd you guess?"

"Just a hunch. I already put her as pending. You don't look at a dog the way Elise looked at Pepper and not come back." She motions for me to follow her. "I already pre-filled most of the paperwork. It's a requirement for accounting otherwise I wouldn't bother."

We stop outside a cage and the smallest little fluffball comes scurrying over. "Elise wasn't exaggerating. She is tiny."

"She's almost six weeks old, small for her breed because she lacked the nutrients she needed until she was found. But she has a clean bill of health." Brynne opens the cage, gingerly lifting Pepper and handing her over to me.

"Isn't she a little young to be adopted?" She barely weighs anything.

"She's eating solid food and everything checks out. She will flourish in a home environment better than here." Brynne gives Pepper's nose a tiny boop and she tries to bite her finger.

Shoes echo on the concrete floor and we turn to see Adeline.

"Young Jae? This is a surprise." She looks at Pepper, her eyes widening a little.

"I want to surprise Elise. You know she hasn't been feeling well lately, and I thought snuggling with a puppy on each side would help. Kimchi would love a friend too." Brynne excuses herself, her expression neutral.

Elise was right about that too—the woman is a vault. You would never guess she knows about the pregnancy.

"She's going to love her." Adeline gushes, leading me back to the front. "I know she hasn't been well. She said she has a parasite."

Coughing back a laugh, I cover my mouth and pretend I'm clearing my throat. "Oh yeah, she should feel better soon."

Adeline takes the paperwork Brynne has ready and hands it over, pointing out where I need to fill out info and sign.

I pay the adoption fee and say goodbye before heading out.

Getting home, I carefully introduce Kimchi and Pepper. Kimchi looks huge compared to Pepper, but after a couple sniffs and Kimchi accidentally knocking Pepper over, they start playing.

I watch closely, but Kimchi tones her energy down, seeming to realize how delicate her new sister is.

When the front door opens, I've just settled the two of them down for a nap. Picking up Pepper, I tell Kimchi to come and we walk to greet Elise.

She doesn't notice the small dog in my hands, bending to say hi to Kimchi. As she stands and catches sight of the gray bundle of fur, she gasps.

"Really?" Her words are choked, and I see her eyes glistening.

Hiding my smirk, I hand over the dog. "I could tell how much she imprinted on your heart and couldn't imagine not bringing her home. Happy pregnancy gift. Is that a thing? If not, it should be."

She tucks herself into me, snuggling Pepper, a wriggling bundle of fur, trying to lick Elise all over. "I'm so happy. Good thing we have like eight months to train her before the baby comes."

We laugh and head into the living room to snuggle our fur babies.

"By the way, it would have been nice to get a warning that you told Rae and Adeline that you have a parasite. I almost choked on my tongue, which should be impossible when you're conscious." Giving her my best glare, I can't hold it in when she starts laughing.

"I totally forgot I said that. It's kind of true though. The baby is surviving on me and my nutrients. Including the calcium in my bones. I just read that today." She shudders a bit. "I think I'm going to stop reading about it so much. Pregnancy is kind of gross when you really explore all it does to my body."

Shaking my head, I chuckle. "I guess you're right, but can we find some other name for the baby other than little parasite?"

"Aww, c'mon. LP is kind of funny. It could be an inside joke." She smirks, her eyes dancing with humor.

"Fine. It seems wrong, but it's funny."

The rest of the week passes in a blur, Elise crashing every night as the first trimester exhaustion continues to hold her hostage. It's hard, not spending the same amount of time with her, but I know she needs to rest, so we make the best of the time we have.

I'm in the kitchen prepping for our guests when Elise comes downstairs wearing a flowy dress, her hair pulled back into a couple braids. She looks a little pale and I don't think it's from having our friends over.

"You okay?" I bring her some orange juice, her most recent craving.

She sighs. "No, the nausea is bad today. But nothing a few saltines shouldn't take care of. I forgot to snack today, so I think my stomach is just a bit too empty."

Turning, I head back to the kitchen and grab her box of crackers. Handing them to her as the doorbell rings, I pull her in for a quick hug. "Eat. I will let them in. It's going to be great."

I decided on barbequing since the smell of raw meat makes Elise's nausea worse. It's also a good chance to get outside while the weather is good.

Opening the door, I greet our friends. They all have different goodies in their arms. Beer, wine, a cake, and Adeline is holding a bag of treats for the dogs.

"Where's the new puppy?" Rae asks, searching between everyone's feet.

Elise comes in, holding Pepper. "Here she is. I didn't want her to accidentally get stepped on."

Rae swoons over Pepper, cooing as Elise hands her over. "Oh my gosh. Aren't you just the tiniest thing?" We all head into the house, chatting noisily as everyone catches up, pouring drinks and handing them out.

As Adeline goes to hand Elise a glass of wine, she takes it, but doesn't drink. Her eyes meet mine and she nods.

"So, we invited you over for an end of season barbeque, but also because we have some news," I start.

Elise licks her lips, focusing on Adeline and Rae. "I'm pregnant."

It's so quiet, you can hear the fridge whirring before the room erupts.

We're surrounded by excited congratulations, and I watch as Rae and Adeline envelop Elise in a hug, with nothing but pure joy on their faces. They hug her and when she meets my gaze, I see happiness radiating from her expression. The last of her hesitation is gone as she starts talking about morning sickness and feeling exhausted.

We have a blast with our friends, eating and talking about how much life has changed. Brynne joins us later after the shelter closes and we celebrate the fact that our little group is growing.

***

The next day we head to my parents for a family dinner. Elise's hands twist in her lap as we pull into the driveway, the last ones to arrive.

"They're going to be ecstatic, don't worry." Reaching over, I squeeze her hand.

She smiles, but it doesn't reach her eyes.

I get out of my car and round it to open her door, taking her hand. She's squeezing so tight I'm pretty sure I'm losing blood flow.

We walk in, and my family sits in the living room chatting. It sounds like things are going well at Ji Hoon's shop and they should be ready to open before the new year.

Elise puts her shoes away, slipping on some slippers before we head toward the chatter.

"You're here!" Ari jumps up, running over to Elise. The two have grown closer since Elise helped get my parents on track to retire. I can only imagine how thrilled Ari will be when we tell them the news.

She drags Elise to the couch and proceeds to talk her ear off about their collaboration.

I give my mom a kiss on the cheek before greeting my dad and brother.

Ji Hoon updates me on what he was sharing. "We finally got our estimates back and booked the contractor—yes, we're using Owen. He's going to start in two weeks once his current project wraps up."

It's not long until dinner is on the table and Ari is going around pouring wine into glasses. When she gets to Elise, Elise covers her glass and politely declines.

Ari's eyes narrow and then, "Oh my god, you're pregnant!"

The entire table freezes, their eyes flying to me and Elise, who looks like she wishes she could melt on the spot.

Reaching under the table, I rest my hand on her bouncing knee. "Well, thanks for that Ari."

She slaps her hand over her mouth, her eyes wide as I don't deny it.

"But you're right. Elise is pregnant. We just found out. She's due in May."

The table erupts into excited chatter. My mom sits quietly, but I can see the sheen in her eyes.

When everyone finally quiets down, Elise looks to my mom, her expression more relaxed, but still a little worried at my mom's silence.

"Elise, you have made us so happy. Anything you want or need, you tell me and we will help. And if you want any special food, you tell me and I will cook." I've never seen my mom smile the way she is currently smiling at Elise. My mother has always wanted to be a grandmother, and I think she lost hope at some point.

Now that hope is a reality.

"Gamsahamnida." Elise thanks her, the tension gone and pure joy radiating from her.

It doesn't take long for the entire town to find out. The excitement is palpable as people stop Elise to ask her how she's doing. I run into Jake a couple weeks after the news breaks and he just turns and walks away. He knows he's at fault for what he lost, hopefully he learns from this and can move on.

As for me, I can't imagine being any happier.

Chapter Twenty-Six

November

Elise

Stroking my small bump, I cross my legs and reach for my phone to call Tash. We've been working together for a couple months and everything is going well. The money from my dad finally came in and I want to offer to invest in her inn.

Dialing her number, I smile when she answers. We've grown fairly close over the past couple of months and Young Jae and I stayed at the inn for a themed Halloween party she held there. I made the treats and she set up a murder mystery. It was a huge success and I think it will become an annual event.

After some pleasantries, I finally get to the reason for my call.

"So, you mentioned some months back that you were looking for an investor. I wanted to discuss the opportunity and offer to invest." My voice is excited. Young Jae and I have talked about it a lot over the past couple of weeks since staying at the inn.

She inhales sharply. "Wow. That's amazing, but—"

"Did you decide against it now?" Frowning, I feel like I remember her still trying to decide her next move right before Halloween.

She sighs, the sound heavy. "No, I signed on with the anonymous person. And I've regretted it ever since, but it's too late."

"Oh no. Are they being weird about the contract?" Concern makes my voice a little sharp.

She takes a shaky breath. "No, I mean the contract was very specific about the role they would take, which is one of the reasons I hesitated to begin with. The investor is Darcy."

It takes me a moment to process. Gasping, my voice is high as I ask, "What? Isn't he the guy who shot you down and then treated you like crap after?"

"The very one. We have getting along issues. And he's always felt I should just sell the inn to him since his family once owned it. It's so misguided. And now I need to run every single thing past him. He's here nearly every day, looking around and making comments." She sounds deflated. "Look, I have to go. I appreciate the offer, but I made my bed and have to lie in it."

We say goodbye and I hang up, disappointed.

Young Jae comes in with some kimchi jjigae, my latest craving.

"You look upset." He frowns.

"Yeah. Tash already signed with an investor, so she had to turn me down. I was just a bit too late and now she's stuck with a douchebag who is an ass to her." Taking the bowl from him, I slump. "I want to do something meaningful with this money, not just spend it on trips and stuff."

He sits next to me, rubbing my shoulders. "We will think of something. You have talked about expanding your own business more. Why not start there? Things are going well with Mary and Nicole at the shop. It might be nice to expand into new areas."

"Well, I have a lot of time to think about it. I won't start anything fresh until after LP comes. I just hope Tash is okay."

"She can hold her own. She's a tough cookie and she won't let him see her feeling down," Young Jae assures me.

After I finish eating, he sets the bowl aside and pulls me into his arms kissing me deeply. "You know what I love most about the second trimester?"

His hands run under the hem of my shirt and I lean into him. "The fact that I have my libido back?"

He lifts me, holding me close as I wrap my legs around his waist. "Exactly."

Epilogue

April

Elise

Young Jae guides me, gravel crunching beneath my feet. The blindfold covering my eyes is disconcerting, but I know that he will not let me fall. Baby girl is due in two weeks and he has been planning this special afternoon for days.

He's been attentive my entire pregnancy, but as we get closer, he's been even more loving and I've never felt more cherished.

We stop and he adjusts me until he's happy before removing the cover from my eyes.

In front of us is the gazebo, looking a lot like that one surprise picnic less than a year ago. Tears fill my eyes, courtesy of pregnancy emotions, and I turn into him, wrapping my arms around his waist.

"This is incredible." My voice trembles with the emotions of how different my life looks from this time last year.

Happiness is a daily emotion and I never dread going home.

We go into the gazebo and he helps me sit on the cushions spread out.

He grimaces a little. "I didn't think this part through. Are you okay?"

Adjusting until I'm comfortable, I stroke my belly. "Perfect, but I will need help up."

His lips twitch. "Of course."

The food before me is simple, my appetite waning the bigger I get. I feel heavy and full all the time. Young Jae dishes up some fruit for me before opening a container of soup. It's a lighter version of kimchi jjigae, something I have been craving constantly.

He sets up a little tray so I don't have to hold everything and sets it before me.

The food is delicious. I barely utter two words until everything he set before me is gone. Glancing up as I set my spoon down, I cover my mouth to stifle a giggle when he looks at me with his brows raised.

"Did you breathe?"

"Of course. It's your fault for making such delicious food available to me." Sighing in contentment, I groan a little as my stomach pangs.

"Do you want more?" He looks concerned as I adjust again, but I wave him off. Every day is uncomfortable.

"No. That was perfect."

He packs all the food away, clearing space before coming to settle in next to me. He's shifting, adjusting pillows around me with an oddly intense look on his face.

"Everything is perfect." I take his hands into mine, giving him a soft smile.

He nods but still looks uncomfortable.

"If I didn't know better, I'd think you were the one who has to push a baby out in two weeks." Rubbing my belly, I feel around to see if I can find baby girl. She stretches, my stomach moving with her.

Young Jae smiles, his hand joining mine as we feel her move.

He licks his lips, looking a little nervous.

I'm about to ask him what's wrong when he starts to speak.

"Elise, I can't believe I get to live a life I never even thought to dream of. Being with you, I've never known happiness like this before. And I want to spend the rest of my life with you. Continuing to build this life together." Young Jae pulls a dahlia out from the basket behind him, in the center is my mother's engagement ring.

Gasping, my heart starts to pound as my eyes shoot to meet his.

"Elise, will you marry me?" His tone is pure love. All nervous energy is gone as he gazes at me, waiting for my reply.

"Yes, absolutely one hundred percent yes." There is no doubt in my mind that he's the person I will spend my life with.

His smile is radiant as he slips the ring on my finger, the fit perfect. When he asked me for it after Uncle George gave it to me, he said it was to put it into his safety deposit box. I didn't want to wear it, not feeling right at the time, but the idea of leaving it in the house was also uncomfortable. I never imagined he would propose so soon, but I did tell him I wanted my mother's ring when we talked about marriage a few months ago.

Young Jae wraps his arms around me, kissing me. My hands twine into his hair, the moment perfect.

He deepens the kiss when I freeze.

"What's wrong?"

"I think my water just broke." The pangs I was feeling and thinking were just normal pains make more sense. I thought they felt more frequent but they have been more annoying than painful.

Glancing down, I grin sheepishly. "That or I peed myself from excitement."

Young Jae barks out a laugh. "Well, let's go just in case."

He stands, bending to help me up before making a quick call. "Hey, Cam, can you please come clean up the gazebo? We might be having our baby early."

The call ends as quickly as it starts. He turns and grabs the hospital bag I missed amongst all the pillows he's spread out so I would be comfortable.

"You brought the hospital bag?" He never ceases to amaze me.

"Of course. It's also why we drove here, just in case." He takes my hand and leads me down the path to the parking lot.

I'm in the car and he's buckled me in, his calm demeanor helping me stay calm as I feel what I now know is a contraction.

"We better hurry, I don't think I peed myself," I grunt out as he starts the car.

His hand reaches for mine, his thumb grazing over the skin as he starts driving.

***

I hold our baby girl in my arms, the love flowing through me like nothing I have ever experienced before. Young Jae sits next to me, half his body hanging off the hospital bed, which can't be comfortable, but I know he wouldn't change anything.

"She's so perfect. And you, you are amazing." He kisses me before looking back at our sweet girl.

We decided to name her Hana. A popular Korean name that also has an English version.

Young Jae's mom peeks her head in, the joy on her face radiating as she comes in, followed by the rest of the family.

"Meet Hana." Young Jae introduces our daughter. He takes her carefully at my nod and hands her to his mom.

She looks up at me, reaching with her free hand. "Thank you for this precious gift."

They all hover near her, taking turns coming to check on me. Ari has a bouquet of dahlias with one daisy snuck in. "To remind you of how far you've come."

We laugh. A year ago, I was miserable and underappreciated. And now I have a family I could only dream of. They were right under my nose the entire time, but I can't imagine the timing being any better.

Young Jae comes over as his family fawns over Hana. "I love you more than I can ever describe." He takes my hand, my mother's diamond glinting on the ring finger, kissing it.

"I love you too."

Opening my arms, I welcome our daughter back and feel complete. Staying with Young Jae was the best decision I could've ever made.

Manufactured by Amazon.ca
Acheson, AB

14550412R00095